THE KINGPIN'S GIRL

-THE GAMES WE PLAY-

TOSHA COSTELLO

Disclaimer

ACKNOWLEDGMENTS

Thank you to my husband and my son. I love you guys.
The two of you are my world. To my new readers and
repeat readers, thank you for your support. I am humbled
and forever grateful.

OTHER BOOKS BY THIS AUTHOR

A LITTLE CREAM IN MY COFFEE

YOU SHOULD BE MINE

UNFRIEND ME

WWW.TLYNCOSTELLO.COM

TABLE OF CONTENTS

CHAPTER ONE

Mia sat at her desk in her home office, talking to her best friend Kayla on the phone. They were going over upcoming wedding plans. She was nervous and excited. A year from now, she would be having the wedding of her dreams. So far, everything was going great. Her fiancé Sean promised to take care of everything. The only thing she had to do was to pick out her dress. Even though the wedding is far off, she wanted to start early. She wanted to have the first pick at things. Only a hand full of people knew they were engaged. They hadn't announced it yet. She was still trying to get over the excitement herself. She felt so lucky to have someone like Sean.

They met at a friend's birthday party. He walked up to her and asked for a dance, and she accepted. They danced the night away and the time slowly passed. That night he drove her home, kissed her on the cheek, and asked her out on a date. He had a way with words. Those words and the way he treated her won her heart. That was two years ago, and he still has a way with words, but in a different way.

"Mia, I'm sending over this link. You have to check out this dress," said her friend Kayla.

"Oh my gosh!" she said with excitement. "I love it! I

need to add this to my list. There are so many dresses that I want. I wish I could have them all!"

"So, are you getting one or two?"

"Just one. You know Sean would have a fit if he knew that I purchased two dresses. We need to go shopping for things to wear on our honeymoon."

"Have you two decided where you want to go?" Kayla asked.

"We've been looking at two places. St. Lucia and Dubai."

"They both sound lovely. You will most definitely need to add a bathing suit to the list of things to get. Along with your shoes for your dress."

"Oh, God! I totally forgot. What would I do without you?"

"I don't know, but if you want to repay me, you can start with buying an extra ticket on whatever trip you choose," said Kayla as they both laughed.

"If Sean was ok with it. Maybe you can come. Who knows? Maybe you will find your Prince Charming."

"No way. I am not looking to settle down right now. You know me and Cedric have been somewhat seeing each other on and off. Maybe he will change?"

"I doubt that," Mia stated right as she heard a door slam, followed by Sean's voice.

"Mia!" he called out.

"Girl, let me call you back. Someone is home, and I don't think they had a good day," she said before ending her call with Kayla.

"Mia!" he called out again.

"Bae, I'm in here," she replied.

"Where's here?"

"Um, in the office." Mia looked up to see Sean standing in the doorway, looking like he's lost his best friend. She got up from her desk and met him where he stood. "What's wrong?" She asked.

"We need to talk," he said as he kissed her on the lips.

"Ok, what is this about? You're scaring me."

"It's not as bad as you think."

"It's the wedding, isn't it? You're calling the wedding off?"

"What? No, no," he said as he grabbed her hand and led her to the living room where they both sat down on the sofa.

For a minute, he said nothing. He sat there, staring into empty space before looking over at her. The silence was killing her. She needed to know what was so important that she had to have a seat.

"What is it? Is it someone else?" She said calmly as she mentally prepared herself for the worst.

"No. It's no one else. I promise. Baby, I um…I lost my job."

Mia only stared at him with a sigh of relief. So relieved that she had to laugh.

Sean looked at her as if she was crazy. What was so funny about losing his job? "Baby, what's funny? Did you hear me? I lost my job."

"Bae, I thought it was something crucial. It's ok. We still have my income, and you still have enough time to find a job. Plus, you will have your severance. So, we're ok, right?"

He didn't know what to say or do. He got up from his seat and began pacing the floor while he was trying to figure out how to tell the love of his life that everything may not be ok.

"We're ok right?" she asked again as her voice began to crack. "Are… we… ok?" This time she stood up and met his gaze.

"I don't know. The severance is gone. There is no severance."

"Wait. What?" She was confused. Most jobs gave out severance. Especially after being there for so many years. "You worked there for over six years. How can this be?"

"There is no severance, ok. There is no last paycheck."

"I don't understand. Maybe I'm missing something here. Did they do away with the severance? This is not adding up. What about benefits like your retirement funds? You know Kayla's brother is a lawyer. I can call him up for advice. There has to be something," she said nervously.

"There's nothing! Ok! Nothing!" He yelled. "I lost my job months ago, ok. I spent everything so that you can have the perfect wedding."

"You what? Wait. Wait. First and foremost, ... I'm not marrying myself. This is our wedding. Secondly, why didn't you tell me this shit months ago?" Mia needed to sit back down for this. She sat there in disbelief with her face in the palm of her hands. She felt like her world was crumbling apart right before her eyes. How could this have happened? They told each other everything.

"Baby, I'm sorry," he said as he seated himself on the edge of the coffee table in front of her. He grabbed her hands and kissed them gently, causing her to look up at him.

"If you lost your job months ago, then where have you been going to each morning?"

"That's the other thing I need to talk to you about," he stated.

"Wow," she said as she pulled her hand away to dab the corner of her eyes where tears were starting to form. She prepared herself for the worst. "What is it?"

"When I lost my job, I searched for a new one. I couldn't find one. So, I......I started working for Anthony."

"Ok. Anthony who? Who's Anthony?"

"You know Anthony, aka Tony Spillane."

"What! Are you crazy? Tony? Doing what Sean!" she yelled as she got up from the sofa. She's heard stories about Tony Spillane but never met him before.

"See, this is the main reason why I didn't want to tell you. I knew you would react this way."

"No! This is the main reason why you should have told me, so I wouldn't react this way! What the fuck do you expect? We're getting married, which is already stressful from planning everything, and now this," she cried.

"I'm sorry," he said as he pulled her into his arms. He stood there, holding her as she cried. He hated to see her cry. If he could take her pain away right now, he would. "We'll still get married, and you can even decorate however you want."

"I don't care about any of that. None of that stuff is important. I just wanted to be married to you," said Mia.

"I'm sorry, baby."

"Whatever happened to open communication? I thought we could talk to each other about anything and everything," she cried.

"We can, that's why I'm telling you now. I just didn't feel right keeping this from you."

"Are we going to be ok?" she asks as she stared at him.

"Honestly, I don't know. We just need to watch our spending. If we do that, we'll be ok. I promise, so don't worry."

Mia looked up at her fiancé and gave a weak smile. He was the love of her life. He was her everything, but somehow, she didn't feel like everything was going to be ok.

"Stop worrying," he said.

"I'm not."

"Yes, you are."

"What about my wedding dress? I haven't gotten my dress yet or my shoes."

"Get whatever dress you want. Don't worry about the cost. I promise I got you, ok?"

She didn't say a word. She just shook her head, ok. "We still need to go over the finances. I know you said everything would be ok, but how can I be for sure?"

"You just have to trust me."

"Ok, I'm trusting you again, but you have to promise not to hide anything else from me."

"Baby, I promise," he said as he kissed her on the lips.

"So, what kind of work are you doing for Tony?"

"Um…well, you know just business," he said as he went to the kitchen with Mia following behind him. He needed something to drink. He knew this conversation was far from being over. So, he settled for a can of beer instead.

"What kind of business?"

"Baby, you don't want to know. Trust me."

"Yes, I do. What am I supposed to tell my parents when they ask?"

"Just tell them I'm a cleaner," he said as he leaned against the counter drinking his beer.

"A what?" she laughed. "A fucking cleaner. Are you serious? How do you go from a manager to a……" She went silent. "Oh, my goodness. Please do not tell me you are doing what I think you are doing?"

Sean said nothing. His look gave the answer to the question she was asking. "It's only temporary."

"I don't care if it's temporary or not. I'm not going to be married to somebody that goes around killing people!"

"I'm not killing people," he replied.

"Yeah, maybe not now, but it's just a matter of time before you're doing that next, or God knows what. What if you get caught? Or what if…what if someone comes after you? What if someone comes after me?"

"No one is coming after you or me, ok? It's only temporary."

"For how long?"

"I don't know."

"Oh great," she said as she threw her hands up in the

air. "Well, since you don't know, let me help you out. You go there tomorrow and let your "BOSS" know that you quit."

"What? You know I can't just do that. It doesn't work that way."

"You're right, silly of me," she said as she smiled. "A job is a job, and you should give proper notice. Give him a two-week notice and then quit. In the meantime, we will figure out something."

"Babe, it doesn't work that way, but ok," Sean said as he took one last swallow from his beer before setting the can down on the counter. He didn't bother to say anything else. He grabbed his keys from the counter and walked out the door.

She knew he was upset, but right now, she didn't care. Just the thought of him working for a dangerous man had chills run up and down her spine. Tony, what the fuck was he thinking? She never met him and prayed that she would never have to.

CHAPTER TWO

Tony was at his desk, smoking his cigar as a woman bobbed her head up and down. Her name was Bianca Moretti. A blonde that he would often call for her service. He enjoyed the good company of a woman, but for some reason, this was getting old. There was nothing fulfilling about getting his cock sucked. Nothing about it screamed romance.

It was just a quick nut for him to bust, but he wanted more. He wanted to come home to a loving woman that he would someday call his wife. He didn't want just any woman. He wanted a woman that could calm him on his worst days and love him despite his flaws. He wasn't perfect by any means, but for the right woman, he would try to be. He wanted a long marriage like his parents. Growing up, his parents weren't perfect, but somehow, they were perfect for each other. His mother stood by his father despite his ways. He often wondered how did she do it? She was a strong mother and still was, and he needed a woman that was strong too. Someone that would stand beside him when the going got tough.

He got up and bent the woman over on his desk. He began pounding her from the back, hoping that it would take his mind off everything. No matter how he tried, nothing was working. He needed more than what this woman or any other woman he fucked could give. He was no fool when it came to these beauties. They all wanted him, but for the wrong reason. They wanted his fame, money, his last name, and his dick.

Tony pounded her as he came. "Alright," he said as he then pulled out of her and discarded the condom in the trash can. "You can leave."

Bianca got up and pulled her dress down, and popped her breasts back in her dress. She began adjusting them so that Tony could see what he would be missing when she left, but it wasn't working. Tony sat in a daze as he smoked his cigar.

"Hey, you gonna call me later, hun?" said Bianca as she took a cigarette from her clutch. She leaned against his desk as she lit the tip and began puffing off it. "You gonna call me?" She said again.

Tony finally looked up and acknowledged her. He said nothing at first as he watched her take several puffs from the cigarette. "You shouldn't be smoking. It's not ladylike, and plus, it's bad for your health."

"Well, isn't that the kettle calling the pot black?" She

took one last puff from it before putting it out on the ashtray that was on his desk. "So, are you gonna answer me or not?" She said as she took a piece of gum from her clutch and began chewing it.

"You know the routine. I'll call you."

"Tony, why you gotta treat me like this?" She said as she began to whine. "Why can't you give us a chance? I'm more than a bed warmer, you know. Do you treat all the girls like this?"

"Questions, questions, questions. You ask too many fucking questions."

"Well, a girl wants to know. I have a lot to offer. I want to be more than just your bed warmer," she said again.

"In order to be a bed warmer, sweetheart, you have to make it to the bed first."

"Whatever Tony," Bianca said as she snatched her clutch from off his desk and stood up. She then looked down at the trash can. If she couldn't get him the old way, she'll just get him another way. "You want me to take the trash out on my way out the door?"

Tony looked at Bianca like she was a damn fool. He was already hip to the game. So, he had to be careful. There was always some twit trying to frame him with a child, but he wasn't buying it. He had one person in mind that he wanted to take to that next level, and the ones he was fucking wasn't the one.

"What? Did I say something wrong?" She asked.

"Leave," he said calmly.

"Fine." She walked towards the door and stopped to give him a piece of her mind. "You know Tony, one day you're gonna wish you had kept all of this," she said as she gestured toward her body. "When that day comes, just hope it's not too late. So, you better take a good look at it now."

"Get the fuck outta here!" Tony yelled as his patience wore off.

"Fucking prick!" she yelled back as she opened the door to leave but ran into one of Tony's boys, Dean O'Brien. "I'm available if you need a good fuck," she said as she then looked back at Tony before leaving. She knew that saying that would get a rise out of him.

Dean O'Brien was Tony's trusted consigliere of many years. He was sharp, smart, and a genius when it came to money-making. He made sure everything that dealt with his business ran smoothly. He was his righthand man, and nothing got past him without Tony knowing it. Tony counted on him to make sure the books were accurate. Every shipment, cargo, or whatever was noted daily. He ran a tight ship and was glad O'Brien was on board to help.

Tony stood at the wet bar washing his hands as Dean entered his office.

"You're hurting hearts again, Tony?" Dean said as he

smiled.

"You're kidding me?" he said as he dried his hands. "She's crazy. Give em' the dick, and they all go crazy," they laughed. "So, what do you have for me? Over the phone, it sounded urgent." Tony took a seat behind his desk as Dean took one across from him.

"You need to take a look at this," Dean said as he handed Tony a black receipt book. "When I went over the numbers for this month, I noticed a page missing."

"You took a page out or something," said Tony.

"Not me, boss, but someone. Thankfully I keep a backup." Dean handed Tony a second black receipt book and pointed to the page that was missing from the other book. "The page that is missing is the same page that had the dates of the next shipment."

"The same shipment that was targeted by the Feds?" Tony said as he sat twirling his pen in his hand while he looked over the books.

"Exactly, but that's not all. I happened to look back through the books and found a few more pages missing. I made a few phone calls, and the numbers on all the pages don't match the total that I received from buyers."

"Please explain," said Tony. He wanted to make sure that what he was thinking wasn't what was happening.

"The money that we are receiving isn't the whole amount. Someone has been taking money throughout the course of time and not just a little. They've taken a whole lot."

Dean kept a book of every transaction that ever took place. The workers would go to collect payments. Each time the money would go to the consigliere before going to Tony. Every gift, payment, loans, or anything else was jotted down meticulously.

"How much is a lot? What are we talking about here? Hundreds? Thousands?"

"Don't shit your pants boss, but we are talking about......thousands," said Dean as he hesitated for a second. He never liked to come baring terrible news. "Sorry, boss. I should have caught it sooner."

Tony said nothing as his mind thought about the newest member they added. Everything was fine until he came along. If he found out that anyone was taking money from him, he would make sure they wouldn't take anything from him again. It's been a while since he had to prove a point. Maybe it was time the old Tony showed the newcomers what he was capable of.

"You have anyone in mind?" Tony asked.

"No one in particular, but I do think you should pay that new guy a visit. Up until he came along, everything was running smoothly. I personally don't trust him."

"I agree. He's bad news for the family. We need to pay him a visit. If he is indeed stealing from me, he will be dealt with accordingly."

"I hear he's a big shot with the lady's too," said

Dean.

"I thought he was with someone. They not together anymore?" Tony asked.

"He is. She's quite lovely too, but I guess he's just a greedy man that doesn't know the meaning of honor."

Tony thought about the woman Dean was referring to. He's only seen her from afar just a few times, and each time she was indeed lovely as ever. She was well put together in every way to be with a loser. He often wondered what the guy did to get so lucky to have her and what can he do to make her his. He now sees that this guy doesn't know the definition of love and honor. It was time for him to step in and do the honors.

"I think it's time we pay him a visit," said Tony as he closed the books.

CHAPTER THREE
TWO WEEKS LATER

Mia was leaving her job after a long day at work. She worked for a large hotel chain here in town as a secretary. She loved her job. It had its perks like attending the company's parties and meeting famous people. It also came with its disadvantages, such as long hours at work and working on the weekend. She couldn't wait to get home to kick off her heels and soak her feet, but most importantly, to discuss the fifty thousand dollars that were deposited into her account. He's given her money before, but never that amount.

"Bae, I'm home," she called out as she entered her home. She hung her purse up along with her black blazer that matched her black pencil skirt and white blouse. "Bae," she called out again, but no answer. She walked into the living room with no sign of her Sean. She thought that was strange. His car was parked outside. Maybe he was in the shower, she thought as she made her way up the stairs. Still, there was no sign of her fiancé.

She kicked off her shoes, undressed, and made her way to the shower. She stepped inside and let the water trickle down her body. Any minute she figured Sean would join her, so she made sure to stay a few minutes just in case. After a few minutes, there was no Sean.

"Sean!" she yells out. She then turned the shower off and grabbed a towel to dry off. She then grabbed another towel for her hair.

She was beginning to worry. She wrapped her towel around her body as she made her way back into her bedroom to call his phone. She looked for her cell phone but forgot that she left it in her purse downstairs.

"Ugh gosh," she said to herself as she dropped the towel from around her body and rubbed on her nightly essentials. She then finished drying her hair and grabbed one of her short robes from the closet. She could hear footsteps downstairs, followed by a door opening and closing. "Sean! Is that you?" she calls out before heading downstairs.

She stopped at the bottom of the stairs. Something didn't feel right. She went to the kitchen to see if he was in there having a beer, but there was no sign of him. Everything was quiet until she heard a noise coming from her office. She could see the light on from down the hallway.

"Bae, I've been calling you," she said as she headed towards the office room. "What are you doing? I've been calling for you since I've been home and…." She started to say but was shaken at the sight of her fiancé tied up and beaten with tape over his mouth. "Oh, my goodness," she cried as she ran to him. "Who did this to you?"

He was trying to tell her something as she began to remove the tape from off his mouth, but she was too late. Someone from behind her grabbed her and placed a hand over her mouth. She screamed and kicked but was no match for the large arms that held her.

"You were certainly right about her boss. She's a fighter," said the guy that was holding her. "You smell nice, honey."

Mia kicked and scream. She was too busy trying to break free, that she didn't see the three other men in there with them. One was sitting in her chair while the other two stood behind him. They were each holding guns. She knew then they didn't come to play games. The one in the chair looked familiar. She looked at Sean and then back at the man in the chair.

"It's nice of you to join the party Mia," said the guy sitting behind the desk. Her desk. He signals for the guy to remove his hand.

"If you scream, you die," he stated as he slowly removed his hand.

"Who are you? What are you doing in our house?" she asked with fear.

"Who am I?" He laughed. His voice was deep, rich, and spoke of authority. "Yo, can you believe this? Who am I?" He repeated as he got up from his seat. He then made his way around the desk and stood in front of Mia. "Who am I?" he repeated, but this time there was no laugh. "I'm the one you will dream about at night. I'm the one your so-called fiancé wishes he would have never messed with. I'm Tony Spillane, your worst nightmare."

Mia was so scared that she couldn't say a word. This was all happening so fast. How could he say he love her and put her in harm's way? She stared at her fiancé then back at the man standing in front of her.

"What do you want?" she cried. Her body was shaking as the tears slid down her cheeks.

"You're too beautiful to cry. Don't worry. I'm not going to kill you," he said as his eyes devoured her body from head to toe. He reached out, touched her face, and wiped away her tears before letting his hand trace her collarbone. He couldn't stop himself as his hand slipped inside of her robe and grazed her nipple.

Sean stared at the man holding his love like he wanted to kill him. How dare he touch his woman! Tony was pissing him off. He was standing way too close and putting his hand where it shouldn't be. He had his chance. Now he sat there helpless. What did he get himself into?

Mia looked Tony in the eyes, letting him know that his touch didn't mean a damn thing to her. "What do you want?" she asked again.

"My money," he replied.

"I don't know what you are talking about. We don't have your fucking money," she said.

"Oh, but you do. You see, that fiancé of yours has sticky hands, and a little birdie told me that money was deposited into your account."

"I don't know what you're talking about. Sean, what is he talking about?"

Tony walked over to Sean and ripped the tape from off his mouth, causing him to yell out from the pain. "Where's my fucking money?" he said calmly.

"Fuck you!" Sean replied.

"Fuck me, huh," he laughed as he turned around and continued laughing like everything was a joke. Then suddenly, his smile disappeared as he took his fist and rammed it into the left side of Sean's face. "Fuck me, huh," he said as he rammed his fist once again into his Sean's face. "We'll see who'll be getting fucked." He looks over at Mia and blows her a kiss.

"Don't you fucking touch her! I don't have your fucking money," he said as he spits out blood. His face was black and blue and was beginning to swell.

"Look, Sean, we can do this the easy way or the hard way. It's your choice," said Tony. After Sean said nothing, Tony reached inside of his black suit jacket.

Mia gasped at the sight of the gun that Tony pulled out from his jacket and began crying. This was it, she thought. She tried to do everything right in her life, and this is how she dies. "Sean, please, just tell him," she cried.

"I think you should listen to your woman here. I'm sure you don't want to leave a beautiful lady alone in this world, just for her to end up with some big dick jock like myself."

"I don't have your money," said Sean. He could barely keep his eyes open.

"Suit yourself." Tony placed the tip of the gun to Sean's head and pulled the trigger, but it was blank. "The next one will be deadly," he stated as he placed the barrel of the gun to Sean's head again.

"Wait!" Mia yelled. "Wait! We'll get you the

money. Just don't kill us. Please," she begged.

"I like her. Not only is she beautiful, but she's smart as well. You let your woman fight all your battles? You have forty-eight hours to have my money. All of it," he said as he stared at Sean as if he was disgusted by him. "Let's go, boys."

Just like that, they were gone. As soon as she heard the door closed, she rushed to Sean with tears in her eyes. "Bae, are you ok? Are you ok?" she asked as she placed both hands on the side of his face. She then got up and ran to her desk for something to cut away the ropes that bounded his hands. "Don't move," she stated as she returned with a pair of scissors and began cutting away.

As soon as he was free, he fell into her arms. "Baby, I'm so sorry," he said as he cringed from the pain.

"It's ok. I got you. We need to get you to a doctor."

"No! No, doctor."

"Ok. Well, at least get you to the bedroom. Can you walk?"

"Yeah, just sore like hell."

"Just lean on me, Ok?"

"Ok."

They took their time slowly walking out of the office. Mia stopped to lock the doors and to get her phone before they continued upstairs. She helped him to the bedroom, where he slowly sat on the edge of the bed.

"I'm going to get a washcloth," she said as she went to the bathroom. She returned with a warm damp towel and began wiping his face. She made several trips until all the blood was off his face. "You have a cut above your eyebrow, and your face is swollen. You need some ice on it. It'll help with the swelling."

"No, I'm good," he said. For a minute, he said nothing. He sat there, holding Mia's hands as she sat beside him. She was his rock, and he was hers. "I'm sorry I got you into this mess. It wasn't supposed to be this way."

Mia wanted to skip the bullshit and get straight to the point. "Today I checked my account, and there was an extra fifty grand in it. I know that's not your money. Is it his?"

He took a deep breath and answered. "Yeah, some of it is his."

"Sean, what were you thinking, stealing from a dangerous man? He could have killed you tonight!" she yelled. She was about to lose it again, but she knew now wasn't the time. "I'm sorry."

"I didn't think he would miss it. At least not right away. Plus, he wasn't going to kill me. He was just bluffing. He was just trying to get us to say something. You should have stayed quiet."

"Seriously? Dammit, Sean! He had a gun to your head. What was I supposed to do? Just stand there and let him blow your brains out?" She said as she pulled her hands away from his.

"I told you he wasn't going to do anything."

"And how do you know that? He scares the living shit out of me. Just thinking about him frightens me," she stated as she went to her dresser and pulled out some gray terry cloths shorts and a white tank top to put on.

"I think you should leave and go stay with your parents for a few days," Sean suggested.

"No! Are you crazy!"

"It'll only be for a few days."

"And tell them what Sean? I'm getting married, and by the way, some guy is trying to kill us? You know my dad will be furious and start an investigation."

Mia's dad spent fifteen years as a patrolman before becoming a Detective. He took pride in his work as he helped solved numerous cases. Like many, he hated crime with a passion and would do anything to protect his family.

"He's not trying to kill us. It's me he's after."

"Wow, that sounds so much better.," she said sarcastically. "I'm not going to leave you."

"It's only for a few days. I think it would be for the best."

"I'm not running away from some overgrown bully. We're in this together."

"I don't want anything to happen to you."

"Really? You should have thought about that before

deciding to go work for the guy Sean."

Mia was upset, and Sean knew this was one of those conversations he wasn't going to win. Every time she gets upset, she would call him by his first name, over and over. Any other time it was Bae. "It's been a long night. I just want to get some rest. We can talk about this tomorrow," he said as he laid back on the bed and placed his hands behind his head before resting his eyes.

"I can't believe you stole the money from him. She waited for him to answer, but he ignored her by keeping his eyes closed and pretending to be asleep. "Sean!" She yelled.

"What! Yeah ok, so what. I fucking took it. What do you want me to say?"

"That you'll take it back."

"What the fuck?" he said as he looked up at Mia. "Now you're just talking crazy. I'm not taking shit back. Do you know what would happen if I walked into his office, trying to return some money?"

"No, but I do know what will happen if you don't," she stated as she placed her hand on her hips.

"I'm not taking it back. It's not that simple."

"How hard is it to go to the bank and get the money out? Better yet, just write a check."

"Mia, it's not that simple."

"Either you take it back, or I will!" she demanded.

"I don't want you going near him. You saw the way he was looking at you. I'll fucking kill him if he touches you again." Sean hoped that it didn't come to that. Killing someone of Tony's caliber would put a target on his head. He'll be setting himself up for a death sentence.

"If you won't take the money back, then I have no choice then to go to my parents and explain to them what's going on."

"Doing that won't help the situation. I told you before, just leave everything to me. I'm the man of this house, and I will take care of it. Trust me. I got this. How many times do I have to say it?"

She looked at him, lying there as if nothing happened. Mia didn't know what to do. She loved her fiancé, but trusting him was the last thing she wanted to do. She trusted him this far and look where it has gotten her. This was her life he was playing Russian Roulette with, and she wasn't about to sit back and watch the house of cards fall apart.

CHAPTER FOUR
TWO DAYS LATER

Mia sat in her car, wondering what went wrong with her and her fiancé. How did they get to this point? They were happy and in love. Now, it's like she barely knows him. He keeps her in the dark with secrets. He's not telling her everything. Well, at least that's what her gut feeling is telling her. Part of her wanted to feel like everything was going to be ok. As soon as the money is returned, they could return to their normal lives.

She checked her makeup and hair in the mirror before exhaling. "Here goes everything," she said as she opened her car door and stepped out. Her attire was normal workday clothes. A fitted button-down shirt, with a dark gray pencil skirt and strappy red sandals. She had to make sure she looked the part for work. She didn't want Sean finding out where she went when she left out the door this morning. She kissed him and said she was off to work. It seems like the roles had reversed. She was the one now lying.

She walked slowly towards the entrance of the tall building. The first floor was a restaurant named Tony's, which was named after him. His office was on the second floor above the restaurant. She assumed it was where he conducted most of his business. She was nervous as she approached the doors. As she walked through the doors, she was greeted by a hostess.

"Welcome to Tony's, do you have a reservation?"

"Um no, I don't. I'm here to see Anthony Spillane," she replied as she stood there nervously.

"I'm sorry, but Mr. Spillane is in a meeting right."

"Could you please call him up and tell him it's Mia Lang. I'm sure he will see me," she said with a fake smile.

The lady gave a lazy smile and picked up the phone to call, just as a bodyguard wearing shades walked up. She placed the phone down and whispered in his ear. He took his shades off and looked directly at Mia.

Mia took a step back when the guy removed his shades. She remembered him. He was one of Tony's men. She was then scared, as she was reminded of the night before.

"Follow me," he said, but she didn't move. "I'm not going to hurt you." He then turned around and began walking away.

She waited for a second as she tried to make her mind up whether she should follow him or not. She wondered if coming there was a bad idea. She should just leave, go home, pack up her things, and disappear. Instead, she decided to follow the guy around the corner where he waited near the elevator. The doors opened, and they both got in.

"You have some nerve showing up here alone," he stated.

"Like I had a choice," she replied.

"There's always a choice," he stated as the doors opened. "This way."

They stepped off the elevator into an open room, dressed in the finest of everything. She glanced around, looking for an exit just in case she had to make a run for it as he led her down the hall towards a closed door.

"Wait here," he stated. He knocked on the door before going inside.

She stood there, holding her breath. This was it. There was no turning back now. "Oh God," she said silently as she stared at her shaking hands. The door opened, and she looked up.

"Good luck," he grinned. "He's waiting for you." He held the door open as she slowly walked inside and closed it behind her.

She was now, once again, face to face with Anthony Spillane. She looked over and saw two other guys standing in each corner. They looked like they were ready to pounce on anyone who dares to lay a hand on Anthony.

"Have a seat. What brings you here?" he asked in a stern voice.

She did as she was told. "I came to bring you your money," said Mia. She was nervous as she looked at the two guys again.

Tony looked at her. He could sense that she was scared and a nervous wreck. He didn't want her to feel as such, not now…not ever. He snapped his finger. "Frankie… Johnny you guys can leave," he stated, and just like that, they left. "Better now?"

"Thank you, Anthony," she replied. She felt a little relief, but she still had to worry about getting out of there alive. They were probably standing by the door, waiting to rush in and end her if that's what he wanted.

"Please, call me Tony," he stated. "So, you came here alone to return what that thief of yours took from me?"

"He didn't mean to. He was just in a bad place and was trying to find an easy way out. I didn't know. I just found out a few days ago. I swear," she said as she reached into her purse and pulled out a check and placed it on his desk. "Here, it's all of the money that was deposited into my account, plus extra."

"There's never an easy way out. Especially if you are dealing with me," he said as he reached for the check and smiled when he looked at it. "What the fuck is this? Is this a joke?" He laughed. "I don't take down payments doll face." Then his smile disappeared.

"What are you talking about? It's all there," she said as she stood up. "That was all that was deposited in my account. That's all I have."

"You're a hundred grand short."

"What? That can't be right. He didn't tell me that," she said with tears in her eyes. She watched him get up from his chair and walked from around his desk until he was standing in front of her. The tears began falling as her heart dropped to the floor. She closed her eyes as his hand was reaching up towards her face. At that moment, she knew this was the end of her, but instead, she felt his hand gently wiping away her tears. She opened her eyes and looked at him.

"He shouldn't have sent you here to clean up his mess."

"He doesn't know that I'm here."

"So, you're not only beautiful and smart, but you're brave as well? You're definitely my kind of woman," he said as she looked away. "Where is this man of yours?"

"I don't know. He was already gone this morning when I woke up. He didn't say where he was going."

Tony didn't say a word. For some reason, he believed her. She was innocent. She didn't deserve some low life like Sean. She needed a real man that knew how to take care of business. In the bed, and also outside of the bed. She needed him.

"What should I do with the two of you? I thought I made myself clear that I wanted my money within forty-eight hours, and here you stand before me with a pinch of it.

"I can get you more money. I just need more time, please."

"I don't give second chances, sweetie."

Mia felt like the world was on her shoulders. How could Sean do this to her? How could he do this to them?

The tears began to fall again.

"You have to stop these tears," he said as he wiped away more tears. This time he wrapped his arms around her.

"What are you doing?" she asked.

He said nothing as he slowly placed a kiss on her lips. She stared at him but said nothing as he leaned in again to devour her lips. He could feel the resistance at first, but then her body relaxed in his arms. He slid one hand down and rested it on her ass, squeezing it as he claimed her lips. Then suddenly she pulls back.

"I'm not supposed to be kissing another man, especially not you. I love him, and we're getting married."

"You might love him, but does he really love you? He's keeping secrets from you. He can't protect you."

"Like you can," she mumbled.

"I have men in place. When I give the say so that man of yours is history. Who will save you then?"

Mia grabbed her purse and stared him in the eyes before walking to the door.

"If you walk out of that door, he's dead, and you're just as good as dead."

Saying those words brought Mia to a halt as she let his words sink in. She didn't know what to do. She needed to think of something quick before it's too late, but who can she trust? The man that loves her or the man that has their life in the palm of his hands.

"What else do you want?" She already knew what

he wanted, but he couldn't have it, or could he? She just wanted him to confirm what she already knew.

"You know what I want," he stated as he came up behind her and stood close.

She could smell his cologne and feel his breath on her neck. She could even feel how hard he was as he was pressing against her. He knew what he was doing, and it was working. "You can have me, but just for a day, but with limitations. When we get you your money and we will get it. You will leave us alone," she demanded.

"And what if you don't come up with the money?" he asked as he placed both hands on her hips and pulled her even closer so that she could feel just how bad he wanted her. He then took his left hand and slipped it inside her skirt and made his way to her spot. He rubbed it gently, causing her body to shiver before sliding her panty aside and slipping a finger inside. He knew it…she was hot and wet. He wanted to throw her on his desk and show her just what she really needed, but he will wait for a more private place. He then pulled his finger out and sucked it until all her juices were gone. "As you were saying."

She must have been holding her breath. It took her a minute for her to catch her breath. She could see now that he doesn't play fair. "If we don't get the money…you can fully have me."

"For how long?" he asked.

"That's up to you," she replied. She couldn't face the man that just almost gave her an orgasm. A man that she barely knew. A man that wasn't her fiancé Sean. "I have to get going."

"For the next three days, you are mine. I will have my guys watching your every move. So, don't try anything stupid," he said as he watched her getting ready to leave.

"Don't worry. We'll have your money."

"We'll see. You better hurry, time is ticking," he said as he tapped his watch.

Mia left and made her way to the first floor and didn't stop until she was in her car. "What the hell did I just do? What just happened?" she said out loud. All she could think of was her life with Sean. How did they go from being honest with each other to a couple that keeps secrets? She hated lying and never wanted a relationship built on lies. How will she tell the man she loves that she made a deal with the devil to save them both? Would he understand?

She could still smell Tony's cologne on her. She needed to get home. Hopefully, Sean wasn't home. How would she even explain coming home smelling like men's cologne that wasn't his? She desperately needed a shower to get rid of his smell and to stop the throbbing urges where she now needed her man, but which one?

CHAPTER FIVE

Mia arrived at her house like a nervous wreck. On her way home, she prayed Sean wasn't home yet, and she was glad her prayer was answered. She rushed in and didn't stop until she reached the shower. She undressed and quickly got in. This was not happening to her. This year was her time to focus on the wedding. Instead, she's focused on trying to think of a way to come up with the money. She hadn't heard from Sean all day. She could only hope that he had some good news.

As the water splashed against her body, all she could think of was the way Tony held her and kissed her. She felt like she belonged in his arms. She felt......safe. She shouldn't be feeling this way about another man, but she does. She was worried about three things. What if they can't come up with the money? What if she enjoys his company too much? What if she has a change of heart about marrying Sean? Her mind was so bogged down with everything she didn't hear her doorbell ring. She turned the shower off and stepped out. She then grabbed a towel and dried off before slipping on a midi white tank dress from the closet. She continued to dry her hair off as she made her way to the front door. She already knew who it was. She texted her best friend Kayla and asked her to stop by and that it was urgent. She could always count on Kayla for good advice. She just hoped that this time wasn't different.

"Hey, girl! What's going on?" Kayla said as Mia opened the door and hugged her. "Are you ok?"

"No, I'm not ok. Come in. I really need to talk to you, and I need your honest opinion.," said Mia as she closed the door behind them. They both had a seat on the sofa where they normally would sit for girl chat. "When I tell you this, please don't look at me differently."

"Oh, my goodness," Kayla gasp. "You're a lesbian?"

"What? No, I'm not a lesbian. I mean, there's nothing wrong with being a lesbian. I have nothing against a lesbian, but no, that's not…I'm not a lesbian."

"Ok, then what's the matter? Your text seemed urgent," said Kayla.

Mia stared at Kayla like she wanted to say something but just didn't know how to say it. She should just say it. She needed to get this off her chest. She had no one else to tell. Someone should know just in case things went bad.

"Mia, just tell me. I'm your girl. Whatever it is, we can and will get through this. I got you.

"Sean lost his job," said Mia.

"Ok, that's nothing bad. He'll find another…."

"He lost it months ago, and he just told me," said Mia

as she interrupted her friend.

"Wow, ok. Maybe he was scared to tell you. You know how men are with their male egos. Don't worry. He'll find another one."

"That's the problem. He found another one working for Anthony Spillane, aka Tony Spillane."

"The Tony?" said Kayla in a shocking tone.

"Yeah. He told me he would quit, and he did, but that's not all of the problems."

"Why do I have a feeling shit is about to hit the fan?"

"Because it has, and it does not smell good at all. Kayla, he took money from the guy. He said he thought Tony wouldn't miss it," said Mia as she explained.

"But he did," said Kayla as she stared at Mia shaking her head yes. "Seriously, what the fuck was he thinking? He is lucky to be alive. My cousin Devin took money from him. Word on the streets says that Tony had him murdered. I don't know how true it is, but I do know he's not one to fuck with."

"Kayla, they came here the other day. They beat Sean up and gave him a black eye. They were going to kill him until I said we would give him the money. Sean deposited fifty thousand dollars into my account earlier that same day. I thought that was all the money."

"Wait a minute. What do you mean, you thought? There's more?"

"He gave us forty-eight hours to get the money to him.

Sean hadn't mentioned a plan or anything to me. So, I took matters into my own hands. I paid Tony a visit today. I gave him a check for fifty-five thousand, and he said it was more."

"How much more?" Kayla asked.

"A hundred grand more," Mia replied.

"You're fucking with me right now. Please tell me you're kidding me."

"I know crazy, right? Now we have to come up with the money."

"I can't believe he gave you guys a second chance. He's not known for second chances, you know."

"Second chances come with consequences."

"Oh, goodness, I'm scared to ask. If I had known that this was some type of soap opera shit, I would have said have a glass of wine ready," Kayla joked. "But, please continue."

"We have a week to come up with the money. He's already given us forty-eight hours, so now we have three days left, and in the meantime, guess what?

"I don't know, but I hope you tell me."

"I'm his."

"His like...his girl?"

"Yeah...pretty much."

"Damn. What if you guys can't come up with the money?"

"Then I'm his for good or at least until he gets rid of me."

Kayla sat there, absorbing everything that her best friend Mia just told her. She was trying to let everything sink in. Her best friend was now involved with a dangerous man. "What does Sean think of everything?"

"He doesn't know that I even went. You know, I kept asking him about paying Tony back every day and nothing. He's not even worried. This is my life he's playing with," said Mia as she began to cry.

"Hey, don't cry. You did what you had to do. I would have done the same thing. Even though you are in a relationship, you still need to look out for you. It doesn't mean that you love Sean any less. It just means that you love yourself too."

Hearing those words put a smile on Mia's face. "You're right."

"Wow, I still can't believe it. You know, as of now, you literally have two men?" said Kayla.

"I don't look at it that way. It's just business and business only."

"Well, whatever you do, don't kiss him on the lips."

"Ok, and why not?"

"Because you will start catching emotional feelings

for him, and you don't want that if you still want your wedding to happen."

Mia's mind glanced back on her visit with Tony. More specifically, his kiss. A kiss that has her wondering, what would it be like in bed with him. She shouldn't want him, but she does in the worst way.

"Hello, are you even listening to me?" asked Kayla as she waved her hands in the air to get Mia's attention.

"Yeah, I'm listening and speaking of listening, thank you for listening to me."

"Anytime, my friend. Are you planning on telling Sean?"

"You know I really want to, but I know he's not going to be happy about it. I don't feel comfortable hiding this from him, and if I do tell him, it could be the end of us."

"Why not? He was comfortable hiding the fact that he lost his job and the amount of money he has stolen. Look, if you want to tell him, then tell him. My door is always open for you. Plus, if you two can make it through the difficult times like now, everything else will be easy to deal with."

"So, should I tell him?" Mia asked.

"Honestly, I don't know. I don't know what I would do if I were in your situation. I mean…you're pretty much going to get fucked either way, and I mean that literally," she said with a laugh.

"There won't be any fucking Kayla. I did say with

limitations."

"Ha!" Kayla laughed. "Limitations? He is going to fuck the shit out of you. Do you really think a man like him will just kiss you on the cheek only or shake hands and say nice doing business with you? I don't think so."

"He did kiss me," said Mia as she looked away. She walked right into this one. She knew her friend, and she knew her well enough to know what was coming next out of her mouth.

"Wow! Oh, my goodness! The suspense just keeps getting thicker. I can't believe I am about to ask this question. How was the kiss?"

"I hate to admit it, but it was nice," Mia said as she daydreamed about the kiss. "That's the part where I feel bad about. I enjoyed the kiss, and I really wanted more. I just feel bad because I'm supposed to get married to the man of my dreams. I shouldn't feel this way."

"This is why you shouldn't have kissed him on the lips, but oh well, the damage is done. All I have to say is be careful. You now know what he's capable of."

"How did I get myself into this. None of this was my fault," Mia said as she closed her eyes. "I'm so tired, mentally, and physically."

"Just get some rest because I have to go. I promised my mom I would come over for dinner later." Kayla gathers her purse as Mia walked her to the door. "Well, I'll talk to you later, friend. If you need me for anything, call me, and please be careful."

"Thanks, I will," said Mia.

They gave each other a hug before Kayla got in her car and left. Mia stood slightly outside her door as she looked up and down the street, wondering if Tony had men watching her every move, but there was no one in sight. She closed the door and rested her back against it. Today was a long stressful day, and she needed to relax, but first, she needed to get started on dinner.

She made her way to the kitchen in search of something to cook. She stood there, staring in her fridge. They had plenty, but with so much going on, her mind was blank. Every time she tried to go on with her day, she kept thinking about Tony and how he made her feel. His touch was so gentle and yet possessive. It was nothing like Sean's touch. Mia stood there until her thoughts were interrupted by the sound of a door opening and closing.

"Bae, is that you?" she called out. "Bae."

"Yeah. Why are you fucking parking in front of the house? You should be parking in the garage," said Sean as he came into the kitchen."

"Well, hello to you too. Where have you been all day?" she asked.

"Here and there," he replied as he threw his keys on the counter.

She leaned over to give him a kiss on the lips like she normally does, but he quickly pulled away to get a bottle of water from the fridge. She found it strange. He never pulls away.

"Did you come up with a way to get the money?"

said Mia.

He laughed as if she'd told a funny joke. "I told you, he'll get his money."

"When?" Mia asked.

"Whenever I get it."

"Sean, this is not a game. It's not ours. It's not yours. I don't want anything to do with this, Sean. You don't know what he's capable of."

"And you do?"

"What is wrong with you? You're putting my life in danger. Are you even thinking of more than just yourself?"

"Of course, I'm thinking about you," he said as he came closer and wrapped his hands around her waist. "Look, he isn't going to do anything. I told you before."

"How can you be so sure?" she said as she wrapped her arms around his waist and laid her head against his chest.

"We're still living. It's day three, and he hasn't done anything yet. I know him well enough to know that if he was going to do something, he would have done it by now."

If only he knew the real reason why Tony hasn't splattered their brains out all over the floor. She's certain he would change his mind then. Maybe she should tell him. He needed to know.

"Are you ok? You suddenly got quiet," asked Sean.

"Yeah, I'm just scared," she said as she pulled away. "I need to tell you something."

He looked at her strangely when she said that. "What do you have to tell me? Is the wedding off? I know I haven't been honest about my job, but I promise you things will get better."

"No, It's not about the wedding. The wedding is still on. I......I just wanted to say that I'm sorry for not cooking dinner two days in a row," she said was a slight smile. She couldn't tell him. At least not right now.

"It's ok baby. I'm going out with the boys tonight to catch a game at the bar," he said as he turned away to walk upstairs.

"You shouldn't be spending money when we have bills. Very big bills. Like the hundred and fifty thousand that you owe Tony." She placed her hand over her mouth. What was she thinking?

He was halfway up the stairs when he stopped. He turned to look at her with anger in his eyes. "What do you mean a hundred and fifty grand?" he asked.

Mia said nothing as she stood there looking at him. She was thinking of ways to quickly recover from what she just said.

"Mia?" He always called her by her name when he was upset. "Who told you that?"

Inside she was freaking out. She figured she would

just throw it back on him. "What do you mean, who told me that? So, it's true? When were you going to tell me? I asked you, and you lied."

"Who told you?" he demanded.

"Don't worry about who told me. Apparently, it's true."

"So, you're going behind my back now? I thought I knew you better than this," he said as he shook his head and continued upstairs.

"Really, Sean!" she yells. "I can't believe this," she said before heading to the living room where she flopped down on the sofa. "Fucking asshole."

About an hour later, Sean returned downstairs, dressed to go hang out with his boys. "I'm out," he said as he made his way towards the front door.

"What time are you going to be back?"

"Don't know, but I'm sure you already know that too." He then walked out the door, giving Mia no chance to reply.

CHAPTER SIX

She awoke hours later after falling asleep on the sofa. She glanced at the clock on the wall and realized it was way past one in the morning.

"Sean?" she called out. She wondered why he didn't wake her. "Sean?"

She searched the house, and there was no sign of Sean. Was he still mad? She reached for her phone on the coffee table and began calling him. His phone rang and rang before going to his voicemail. She tried texting him and no reply. She didn't want to be the crazy fiancé constantly calling him, but she also feared that something might have happened to him. After all, he was on Tony's hitlist. He always called her, but not this time. She tried calling and texting him one last time before grabbing her things and leaving out the door.

She drove in silence as she made her way to the bar where Sean was supposed to be at. She glanced around the parking lot, searching for his car. With no sign of it, she decided to find a parking space instead. The parking lot was packed with cars, but most were bikers. She reached into the backseat and grabbed a light jacket to cover up with and doubled checked her appearance before getting out of the car. She clenched her jacket closely as she made her way inside. Her eyes scanned every corner of the room in hopes of seeing her fiancé.

"Excuse me," she said as she made her way through the crowded room and took a seat at the bar. The air was filled with cigar smoke and the sound of people bickering and yelling at the losing football team playing.

"Can I get you something?" The bartender asked.

"A Margarita, please," she replied.

"Coming right up."

Mia searched every corner with her eyes again, hoping to see Sean, but there was still no sign of him. He was supposed to be there with his friends. She wasn't the type to chase after a man, but with everything going on, she just needed to make sure Tony didn't change his mind.

"Here you go," said the bartender.

"Thank you," she replied as she took her drink. She hated dining out alone. Nights like this, she would either be with Sean or with Kayla, having fun. There was nothing fun about sitting alone, hoping your fiancé was still alive in one piece.

"Excuse me, is this seat taken?" said a male voice.

"No," she replied.

The guy smiled and introduced himself. "I'm Barry."

"Hi Barry, I'm Mia."

"How about I buy you a drink?" he asked.

"No, thank you. I have one already." She kept her conversation short. Hopefully, he would get the clue that she didn't want to be bothered.

"How is a beautiful woman such as yourself sitting all alone?"

She smiled. She knew his type too well. The kind that looks all innocent, but in reality, they were all jerks. The ones that play the Mr. Nice Guy role all too well and the ones that try to sweet-talk their way into girl's pants are usually the ones she always stayed away from. She didn't have to worry about anything anyway because she was already taken.

"I'm here with my fiancé. He just stepped away for a few seconds." She lied, but only to hope that Sean would see her and come over. "He'll be back real soon."

"Well, we both know that's not true."

"Excuse me?" said Mia as she stared at the stranger.

"I've been watching you since you walked in. How about we go take a ride back to my place," he said while placing a hand on Mia's thigh, but she quickly removed it.

"Don't you dare touch me!" she yelled. She grabbed her drink and tried to move to another seat but was stopped when Barry grabbed her arm. The bar was so loud and busy that no one even noticed what was going on.

"Hey, where are you going?" said Barry as he tightened his grip on Mia's arm. The more she tried to pull away, the more he got angry and tightened his grip even more.

"Look, I told you I have someone. Now get your filthy hand off me or else." Mia knew she couldn't handle the guy, but she always took her trusted friend, her mace with her, and she wasn't afraid to use it.

"Or else what?" He stood there with all smiles like shit was funny.

"Or you fucking die," said another male voice behind Mia. Barry quickly took his hand off Mia.

When she turned around, her night just got interesting. It was one of Tony's bodyguards. The same one she met before at her house and at the restaurant. What did he want with her?

"I'm sorry dude, I didn't know she was with someone," said Barry before taking off through the crowd.

Now that that's over with, he turned his attention to Mia. "What the fuck are you doing here this late?" he said. "If Tony catches you here, he'll be pissed.

"I came here looking for my fiancé. I haven't heard from him. He said he would be here. Do you know where he is?"

"Don't worry. He's not dead. At least not yet," he said as he laughed. "I haven't seen him."

"I don't get it. He said he was going to the bar to watch the game with some friends."

"He's not who you think he is."

"What do you mean? What are you talking about?" Mia asked curiously.

"It's not my place to tell," he said as he reached behind the bar and grabbed a glass, and began filling it up with beer from the keg.

"What are you doing?" she asked.

"What does it looks like I'm doing? I'm getting a beer."

"I know that......never mind." She just shook her head. He was a big buff guy. She doubted if anyone would say something to him. Apparently, this wasn't his first rodeo. "I want to say thank you for earlier, with the guy."

"I did what I was supposed to do," he said as he took a big sip from his drink.

"Excuse me? What do you mean you did what you were supposed to do?"

"No one lays a hand on Tony's girl. No one fucks with anyone in the group. We protect what's ours. That asshole is lucky tonight. It could have ended badly for him."

"First of all, I'm not Tony's girl. Secondly,

well…… never mind." She wanted to know what he meant by it could have ended bad for Barry, but she had an idea. "I'm not Tony's girl. I barely know him, and plus, I have a fiancé."

He looked at her like she was crazy. She really didn't have a clue. Once Tony claims you, you're his, but once you're disloyal to him, you're dead. He was picky when it came to women. Everyone knew it. So many women wanted Tony, but he didn't want them. What he wanted was Mia, and she was in for the ride of her life. Her time with Sean was ending, but she just didn't know it yet.

"We're about to close Miss," said the bartender.

"She's good, Joey. She's with me."

"You must come here a lot?"

"Yeah, when I have the chance."

"You know, I don't even know your name. We got off on the wrong foot. You know mine, and I think it's only fair that I know yours," she insisted.

"It's Salvatore, but everyone calls me Sal," he said without hesitation.

"Thanks, Sal," said Mia, but he didn't respond back. He sat there, drinking his beer.

"It's late. You should get going," he said.

"I told you, I'm looking for my fiancé. He said he would be here with his friends, so I want to wait."

"I've been here all night, and I haven't seen him. You should go home."

"I'm not going home."

"I told you, your man isn't here. This place isn't for nice women like yourself. If Tony finds out that you were out this late surrounded by a bunch of frazzled men, he will be furious."

"Stop saying that. He's not my man. I have a man, ok?"

"Yeah ok. Look, ask yourself this question. Why would he come to a bar he knows Tony owns? If he was your man, he wouldn't keep you in the dark."

"Since you know so much, why don't you just tell me? Save me some time."

He laughed at her question. "That's not my place to tell you. I don't step on anyone's toes. Just ask your man."

"I will ask him when I find him," she said as she sipped the last drop of her drink.

"I'm not talking about that loser. I'm talking about your new man. If you want to know what's going on, check with him. Just know that your old man is a thief. That's all I'm saying."

Mia didn't say anything else as she got up from her seat and left. That talk with Sal changes everything. She had no idea that Tony owns the bar, but after hearing Sal talk tonight, he was right. Sean was hiding something from her. She didn't know what it was, but she was going to find out. Another problem added to her list. Problems that Sean just keeps making. Who was this man she was marrying?

CHAPTER SEVEN

It was the weekend as Mia awoke the next morning. She looked over to see no Sean in her sight. She then looked at her phone, and there was no phone call or text as well from him. She was angry. How can the man that claims to love her act this way? This isn't the man she fell in love with. The man she fell in love with wouldn't lie to her or put her life in danger.

She started her morning as usual before heading downstairs. She heard movement in the kitchen, causing her to stop at the bottom of the stairs. She wasn't taking any chances as she grabbed an umbrella that was sitting nearby.

"Sean?" she called out as she slowly moved closer.

"Yeah, baby," Sean replied from the kitchen.

She took a deep breath as she placed the umbrella down. She stood in place for a few minutes, trying to control her anger that was building up. The anger from last night after finding out that he wasn't where he said he was going to be. He was seriously making it easy to become Tony's girl. She made her way to the kitchen, where she could smell the goodness that he prepared for them.

"Good morning, baby," he said as he greeted her in the doorway with a kiss upon her lips. "I made your favorite ham and cheese omelet with a side of breakfast potatoes." He guided her to the table and pulled out her chair. He took his seat across from her and poured them both orange juice into a glass.

Mia was enjoying this side of Sean, but it was something out of the ordinary. She grabbed her fork and cut into her breakfast. The first bite was heavenly, followed by the next.

"How did you sleep?" he asked.

"I slept, ok."

"What did you want to do today?"

"Don't know," she replied, keeping all her answers short. Today just wasn't the day. How could he just sit there and act as nothing happened?

"You ok? It seems like something is bothering you."

"Really?" Hearing that brought a smile to her face, but not a good smile. It was more of a sarcastic smile that was hiding how she really felt right about now.

"What? What's so funny?" he asked.

"What's funny? Do you really want to know what's funny, Sean?" She placed her fork on her plate and looked directly at him. This time, there was no smiling taking place. "You know, it's funny how you can just sit here and act as nothing happened."

"I don't know what you're talking about," he said as he got up from his chair and carried his plate to the sink.

"Really? So, you didn't come in super late last night?"

"Baby, I came in, and you were asleep. I didn't want to wake you, so I slept downstairs in the guest room."

Mia jumped up from her chair with anger. She was tired of his lies, and they weren't even good lies. How dare he have the audacity to sit there and lie to her face. "So… you were at the bar all night?" she asked as she stood there with her hands on her hips, tapping her foot.

"Yeah, I told you that already."

"With your boys?"

"Yeah, me and the boys. What are you getting at?" he said as he watched her closed her eyes and exhaled. He walked closer to where she stood and held out his hand for her to take it.

She stared at his hand before looking up at him. "You were there all night?" she asked again calmly. "I tried calling you and texting you. Why didn't you answer the phone?"

"I didn't hear my phone, and plus, you know the reception is bad in parts of that bar. I promise I was there. You can even call my boy up. He'll tell you." He reached into his back pocket, pulled out his phone, and handed it to her.

Mia slapped the phone out of his hand, causing it to fall on the floor. "No, thank you." She didn't care if it was broken or not.

"What was that for?"

"You know, there are two things I can't stand. I can't stand a liar, and I can't stand a thief and apparently... you are both. If we are going to make us work, we need to be honest with each other." She felt bad for asking him to be honest with her when she was hiding a secret from him too.

He picked his phone up and placed it back into his pocket. "I'm telling you the truth. If you think I'm lying, then call."

She already knew the routine. She didn't need to call anyone because he probably already had his friends to cover his whereabouts. "I don't need to call anyone Sean. I was there."

"What the fuck do you mean you were there? So, you're checking up on me?"

"Of course not! After trying to reach you, I decided to go to the bar myself. With everything that's going on, I wanted to make sure you were ok. So yeah, I got up and went there myself, and you know what I found? I found out that you weren't even there and haven't been there all night."

"I was there," he argued as he left her standing there. He took a seat on the sofa and turned the tv on, blasting the volume up, hoping to drown out their conversation.

"Why would you go to a bar that belongs to the same man that you despise? The same man that you stole from. Remember? The last time I checked, you two weren't the best of friends."

Seeing that this was a never-ending battle, he then began texting someone on his phone before getting up to put on his shoes. "Some things are better left unsaid."

"Really? Is that all you have to say? What's going on with us? We are supposed to be happy and in love. We're supposed to have each other's back. How did we even get to this point?" she cried. "I feel we are slipping away from each other. All because of the money. Money that you didn't even have to take."

"I did what I had to do to keep a roof over our head and to make sure you had everything you ever wanted and needed. That way, you wouldn't run to your parents asking for money."

"Excuse me. Is this what everything is about? When have I ever asked them for money?" she asked but received no response as she watched him begin to walk away. "Talk to me! Stop running away, dammit! What have I done to be treated like this?"

Sean looked at Mia before looking at his phone. "Since you are so good at assuming things and making me look like the bad person, I will leave the questions for you to figure out." Once again, he left her standing there with no explanation.

"Where are you going?" she cried.

"I'm going to take a fucking shower, alone!" he yelled out.

She was tired of his games, tired of being left out and tired of his attitude. Solitude was beginning to take a toll. The way things were going, they won't be together soon. Maybe this was the reason her parents disapproved of their relationship. Maybe they knew something she didn't. She wiped her tears as she stood there. There was no time to cry. She still had to figure out how to come up with the money, but in the meantime, she might as well enjoy her weekend off alone or at least try.

She followed Sean upstairs. She could hear the water from the shower. She wanted to join him, but he insisted that he wanted to shower alone. She should listen to him, but she just wanted to kiss and make up. She hesitated for a minute before dropping her clothes to the floor. He's mad now, but there's nothing a little makeup sex couldn't fix. After all, make-up sex was the best sex.

She made her way into the bathroom, where she could see the outline of his body through the foggy glass. He was one fine piece of specimen. He took care of himself, which was one of the attributes that she loved about him. She placed her hand on the shower door, opened it, and got in. His back was facing her as she walked closer and placed her hand on his back.

"Sean," she said softly. "Sean, I'm sorry. Can we just talk about it later?" she asked as she then placed her arms around him and relaxed her body against his. She smiled as she felt his hands on hers, but it slowly vanished when she felt his hands push her hands away. He didn't bother to look at her as he slid past her, leaving her standing there in disbelief. "Really, Sean?" she said in disbelief before breaking down in tears. She cried her heart out as she slid down onto the shower floor.

This was the first time Mia has seen Sean act like this. The first time he ever rejected her, and it hurt. She hated seeing him like this, but it wasn't her fault. She just wanted answers and wanted everything to be over with so they could go back to living their normal lives. She sat there in the shower for a few minutes before deciding to stop feeling sorry for herself. She got up, turned the water off, and grabbed a towel from off the towel bar. She wrapped it around her small waist and waited for Sean to leave the bedroom. She didn't want to see his face right now. She was done trying to talk to him. It was time for her to take matters into her own hands.

As soon as she heard Sean leave out of the bedroom, she made her way out of the bathroom. She went straight to the closet to look for something to wear. She needed an outfit that made a statement and an outfit that was meant for a pleasurable business. She settled on a fitted plum-colored short skirt with a sleeveless mauve shirt that hugged her neck and revealed just a little cleavage that peeped through the opened slit. She stood in the mirror as she took her messy hair from out of a bun and let it fall to her shoulders to dry. She ran her hands through her hair to loosen up the curls before applying her makeup. She didn't want to look at him, so she then glanced out the window to make sure he was gone before she gathered her purse and left the house. She was going to get to the bottom of Sean's secrets.

She drove with one place in mind, and that was Tony's.

CHAPTER EIGHT

Mia sat in her car, debating if she should go in Tony's or not. She was prepared to say whatever was on her mind, but now that she was here, she wasn't sure of what to say. This wasn't her first run-in with Tony, but she was sure nervous as hell. Who wouldn't be? He was notorious. She knew little about him but knew that he wasn't the one to fuck with. So many things went through her mind, but she had no choice. Running to her parents would just upset Sean. She had to do what she had to do.

She grabbed her purse and exited her vehicle before making her way towards the restaurant. The door was held open by a gentleman that couldn't keep his eyes off her.

"After you," he said as he watched her walk in. He already knew who she was, but it still didn't stop him from looking. Tony made sure everyone knew she was with him.

"Thank you," she said but kept looking straight ahead. She didn't want to get into another argument with another man, just to have one of Tony's men come to her rescue again.

"You're welcome sexy," he said before disappearing around the corner.

"Hi, I'm Angela. Welcome to Tony's. Do you have a reservation?" said the hostess.

"Oh, I'm sorry. I don't have a reservation."

"No problem. Let me check," she said as she left her station and returned a few seconds later. "I'm sorry we are full, but I can put your name on the waitlist."

"Umm, sure," she said hesitantly. "How long is the wait?"

"It will be at least a thirty-minute wait. We have been extremely busy. What's your name?" she asked.

"It's Mia Lang," she said to the hostess.

The hostess looked up from writing. Her demeanor changed from being sweet and professional to disgusted. "Mia Lang?"

"Yes, is there something wrong?" Mia asked curiously as she stared at the hostess.

"No," the hostess replied as she grabbed a menu. "Follow me."

Mia thought that was strange. How did a thirty-minute wait turn into a one - minute wait? She didn't bother to ask. Maybe today was her lucky day after all.

She followed the hostess to a private booth in the corner overseeing the entire room. She stepped up into the booth and took a seat. For a moment, she felt special until the hostess slightly threw the menu down in front of her.

"He's just using you. You're not his type," said the hostess as she looked Mia up and down.

"Excuse me?" Mia replied.

"You heard me. You're not his kind. He's not into African Americans. You get the special treatment until he gets the goods. After that, he'll toss you aside like the rest. Either dead or alive," she whispered. "Your waiter will be with you shortly," she said with an attitude before turning to leave.

Mia sat there, confused. Why would the hostess say such words to her? Did she also know something that she didn't? She took the words dead or alive as a sign that she shouldn't be here.

"What was I thinking?" she said to herself as she stood up, reached over, and snatched her purse off the seat. She was in such a hurry that she didn't notice her reason for being there standing at her table. She gasped at the sight of him.

"Leaving already?" Tony asked as his eyes roamed her body. He enjoyed seeing her bending over but also enjoyed the sight of her breast when she turned around. He wanted to see more, but only in due time.

"I um…something came up," she lied as she stumbled on her words. She found it hard to look at him, but she had to. She wanted to show him that she wasn't afraid of him.

"Sit," was all he said as he gestured towards the booth.

She did as she was told. Not because she was afraid, but because she didn't want to start a scene. This wasn't the place for it. He probably had men stashed all around the building, just in case something went down. A guy like him you couldn't run from. There was no hiding.

"How did you know I was here?" she asked as he moved closer. She could feel extra eyes on her as she looked over to see the hostess staring at her. The hostess was making sure Mia knew she was watching her.

He rested his arm on the seat behind her. "I know everything. No one comes in here that I don't know. Especially anyone as beautiful as you."

Mia wanted to play along and give that hostess something to watch, but she had more important things to do. She needed to find out what was really going on so she could save her relationship.

"Why are you here? Miss me?"

"Don't flatter yourself. I just wanted to have lunch," she replied.

"Of all the places to have lunch, you decided to come here?" He said as he stared at her. She said nothing.

"Can a girl just treat herself to lunch?" she said as she stared back.

"Not alone looking damn sexy. Sean doesn't deserve you. Soon he will realize it."

"Well, actually, that's what I'm here about. I want to know what it is that he's hiding from me. I try to talk to him, but I get nowhere. I know he's hiding something. I was hoping you knew something."

Tony could see the worry on Mia's face. He wanted Sean dead but spared him this long because of her. He knew she was different from the rest. There was something about her that made him trust her.

"How did a good girl like you end up with a loser like him?"

"He's not a loser," she frowned. She and Sean may not be on the same page right now, but she will be damned if anyone talked bad about him. "He's a good guy who made an honest living. He just got caught up with the wrong people."

"Good guys don't steal. Sean...he's a liar, thief and a rat," he implied.

"What do you mean by a rat?" She had an idea of what he was referring to, but the Sean she knew, wasn't a rat. Maybe he meant something else?

"Word got out that he's trying to frame me. I'm a businessman. I have friends in very high places, so nothing gets past me. When Sean came to me for work, I trusted him and gave him work. He took my money and used it for some drug trade that he's running. On my territory!" The more he talked about it, the more he was getting fueled. "He hid drugs on my cargo. He tried to set me up. I don't deal with drugs."

She gave him that look as if she didn't believe his story about not being a drug dealer.

"What? You think I deal with drugs? I might be a

66

lot of things doll face, but a drug dealer isn't one of them," he insisted. "They bring too much attention from the Feds. I like attention, but not that kind of attention. Maybe you can give me some attention real soon."

Mia ignored his last comment. She didn't want to waste valuable entertaining that thought. "How do you know it was him? I mean...it could be anyone?"

"Is that what he's telling you?"

"Look, whatever happened, I'm sorry......" Mia's words were cut off when the hostess Angela made a stop at their table.

"Excuse me, boss, but I need a word with you," she said as she chewed her gum. Her nose was turned up as she glanced at Mia.

Tony slowly looked at Angela as if she said something wrong. "Do you not see me busy?"

"Yeah, but I still need to talk to you. It's important. More important than this here."

Hearing the way Angela spoke about Mia made Tony furious. No one disrespects her, especially in front of him. "Her name is Mia Lang, and if you ever disrespect her again, I will make you disappear faster than you can blink. Now get outta here!" he said with anger.

Angela gave Mia a snare before storming out of sight. Her shift wasn't over, but she was leaving anyway. They watched her leave out in a hurry, giving Mia a sense of relief. Today wasn't the day to fuck some bitch up, but she will if needed.

"I don't think she likes me much," Mia stated.

"Who, Angela? She doesn't like anyone much, not even herself," he replied.

"So, tell me, where can I find out where Sean conducts his business?" Mia asked. "If what your saying is true."

"You don't know?" he asked.

"No. I told you he doesn't tell me anything."

He laughed. "Why are you marrying him?"

Mia looked away. She wanted to tell him how she really felt but feared she wouldn't leave out of there alive. So instead, she kept her mouth shut and her feelings to herself. "Because I love him."

He laughed at her words. "Love. What is love if there's no honor behind it? A time will come when love is tested. When that day comes…choose wisely," he said as he stared at her.

"I should get going," she said as she got up from the table, but not before Tony grabbed her arm, pulling her back down.

"Look, he's not the man you think he is. You'll learn soon doll face," said Tony.

"And you are?" she said quickly.

"Don't ever compare me to that druggie of yours! You tell that loser to make sure he has my money, and if I catch him on my territory, he's dead. Then you'll be all mine, for good," he said as he stared at her chest. His mind lingered on the last time she was in his office and how good she tasted. He wanted more. In his mind were images of all types of things that he wanted to do to her. She ought to be glad they were in the open. If they were alone, she'd be singing a different tune.

After hearing those words, Mia left immediately. She could feel his eyes locked on her. She didn't stop walking until she reached her car. She didn't want to believe everything he said about Sean. She's known him way longer than Tony has. If Sean was dealing with any kind of drugs, she would know. Would she?

CHAPTER NINE

After stopping at a few stores, Mia finally made her way home. She sat in her car, just thinking about what Tony said. The part about her being his was a joke. She wanted to laugh. She will never be his. Even if the deal falls through, her heart will never belong to him. In the meantime, she had a plan.

Hours later, Mia laid on the couch as she heard the front door open. She knew it was Sean, so she didn't bother to open her eyes. She pretended to be asleep to save them both an argument. After being rejected, she didn't really know what to feel anymore, but somehow, she still loved him. This was just a phase that they were both going through. They just needed to make it through it. She laid there with her eyes closed as she heard Sean call her name.

"Hey Mia, wake up," he said. "Mia!"

She wanted to remain asleep, but he seemed as if he wasn't giving up.

"Mia, wake up!" he said as he became louder.

This time she gave in. "Hey," she said as she pretended to have just woken up. "How long have you been home?"

"I just got home, but let's not talk about me. Let's talk about you," he said as he stood over her.
"What? What about me?" she asked as she sat up.

"Oh, so you want to play dumb now?" he laughed.

"Sean, what are you talking about?"

"I'm talking about you having lunch with the enemy. You trying to leave me for him or something?" he said as he paced the floor.

She didn't know what to say. She could tell he was upset. He wasn't supposed to find out. How did he know? Did he have someone spying on her? She needed a lie and needed one quick, but then again, why lie. That's what got them in this situation anyway.

"Babe, I went there to have lunch. That was it," she said as she stood up.

"I'm supposed to believe that shit? You went there to have lunch and ended up at a special table, his table with him," he said as he slowly walked towards her until he was standing in front of her.

"I swear that's all that happened. He saw me there and had a seat. I ended up leaving and went shopping," she said as she pointed to the bags on the chair. She didn't feel like going upstairs, so she ended up putting on some tights and a t-shirt from the dryer. Plus, she didn't want Sean to see what she wore. "Babe, I wouldn't do that to you. You should know me. We're in this together. I love you."

She waited for him to say it back, but he said nothing. Instead, he went to the kitchen and grabbed himself a bottle of beer. She couldn't wait for everything to be over with. She wanted her man back.

"What did he want?" he asked as he stood in the kitchen doorway.

"He didn't want anything."

"Is that right."

"Yeah. Well, he did say that you are not the man I think you are."

"And you believe him?"

"Sean, I honestly don't know what to believe."

Hearing that pissed him off. He knew Tony was a vicious man, but to talk down at him just to get Mia wasn't happening. "You know he has his eyes on you. He wants you. He'll say anything to get you."

"Well, he can't have me." She wanted to go wrap her arms around him but was afraid he would reject her again. She couldn't take any more rejections. She wanted to feel his arms around her. Instead, she had a seat on the arm of the chair and wrapped her arms around her waist.

"You need to stay away from his bar, his restaurant, and anything that consists of him. Most importantly, stay away from him. He's a fucking vicious man that doesn't care who he hurts. I don't want you involved in any of this."

"You involved me when you decided not to involve me. Things could have ended up differently, and they still can. Just fill me in on what's going on with you and with us."

"Some things are better left unsaid."

"What is that supposed to mean? That's the second time you've said that."

"Don't play dumb, Mia. You're smarter than that. It means what it means."

"You're something else, Sean. You know that, right? What happened to you?" she asked as she grabbed her shopping bags and went upstairs.

She didn't wait around for him to respond. She was tired and was going to bed. Tomorrow was a workday for her, and she needed all the rest that she could get. She was happy to have the weekend off finally, but since so much has happened, she'd rather be at work.

She then dropped her bags near the closet and headed straight to the shower. The water poured down on her as she took a deep breath. She was tired. Not physically, but mentally. Just thinking about everything was exhausting and overwhelming. She wanted this to be over with. She could easily call her parents, and things would go back to normal, but not with Sean.

After a few minutes of showering, she turned the water off and grabbed her towel. She dried off and began doing her nightly routine of getting ready for bed. She then checked her phone. No missed calls or text, which was a good thing. She tossed herself on the bed and closed her eyes. She thought about the plan she had in mind but decided against it.

Sean didn't want her to get involved with everything. She wanted to trust that he will fix everything, and that's what she was going to do. He was still home. Hopefully, he would come to bed, and they would make love like before. She could hear his footsteps as they got closer. The door opened as he came in. He didn't stop until he reached the shower.

She could hear the water running as she patiently waited for him to get out. It was only a short time, but it felt like an eternity. After several tries, she positioned herself in a sexy pose slightly lying on her side and stomach with her short white gown raised up even higher. She positioned her ass up just a little and pretended to be asleep. She had her ass facing the doorway so that it would be the first thing he saw when he entered the room.

It was going on almost three weeks of no touching, no kissing, and no sex. The last thing she remembered was Tony's touch. The way he kissed her, touched her, and the way he had her body trembling. She wanted him to stop, but her body was saying something totally different. It was like her body had a mind of its own.

Her thoughts were interrupted as she heard movement and the sound of pants zippers. She turned around to see him getting dressed. "Where are you going?" she asked.

"I have business to take care of," he said as he continued getting dressed.

"What kind of business?" She knew asking that question could start an argument, but she needed to know.

"Business? What did I tell you about being all up in my business?"

"I'm sorry ok. It seems like it's been months since we actually spent time together."

"Because every time we do, we argue. Just like now."

"We're having a discussion, not an argument. Plus, I have the right to know. You're my fiancé remember, or have you forgotten?"

"I gotta go," Sean said as he looked in the mirror.

"Well, can I go with you?" she asked.
He laughed. "You know you can't go with me," he said as he left out of the room.

"Oh really, we will see," she mumbled to herself. It looks like her plan was back on. She waited until she heard the door closed before running downstairs. She slid the first pair of shoes on that she saw, which was a pair of black flipflops.

She then waited until he was at the end of the driveway before sneaking to her car. She knew she had to be careful and not get caught because getting caught could mean the end of them. "Alright, Sean let's see where you've been hiding," she said out loud as she drove. She made sure to stay a car length behind so she wouldn't get caught.

After driving for almost twenty-minutes, he finally came to a stopping point. It was an old, abandoned building that she didn't recognize. She parked across the way, out of sight, and killed the engine. "That was easy. All those James Bond movies were finally kicking in," she joked.

She turned off all the lights in her car, so she wouldn't draw attention as she opened her door. Just as she opened her door, she looked down at what she had on. She still had her white gown on. She wouldn't be able to blend in easily with white on. Then she remembered she always kept a spare jacket in her car. She glanced in the back seat and prayed it was still there, and it was. Tonight was her lucky night. She grabbed it and quickly put it on before exiting her car. She softly closed the door as she dashed across the street.

She saw a large garbage can and hid behind it, so she wouldn't be seen. "What is this place?" she thought to herself. She looked around to make sure no one was around before moving closer to another large garbage can. She couldn't see what was going on, but she could hear several voices coming from inside. The voices appeared to be both male and female voices.

"I know that voice," she thought to herself. That voice sounded like the hostess's voice from Tony's restaurant. She could hear females laughing and men talking. One voice stood out, and that was Sean. Why was he here inside an abandoned warehouse instead of being home with her?

She needed to get closer so that she could have a look to see what was going on inside. She wanted to know what she was getting herself into and who she was about to marry. There was a window nearby, and she needed to get to it so that she could see inside. She was careful not to disturb the trash on the ground, she needed to make sure to keep quiet. She looked around before making a dash to it. She placed her back against the wall and gave a sigh of relief. Even though she had nothing to hide behind, her view was ten times better. She could see what was going on as she kneeled and glanced through the window.

Four women were naked sitting at a table with what seemed to be drugs. They were weighing, measuring, and packaging each baggy carefully before weighing it again. She was speechless. Tony was right. Her heart sank to the floor when she saw Sean with someone familiar. He kissed her on the lips and gave her a hug. Could it be innocent? The hug was lasting way longer than Mia wanted it to. She didn't know what to feel, hurt, or disappointed. She just knew one thing she was tired of hiding.

She ducked past the window and eased up from off the ground. She didn't know what she was going to say when she confronted him. She only knew it wasn't going to be nice. "Tired of being the nice one," she said to herself right before she felt a cold piece of metal at the side of her face.

"Going somewhere?" A male voice said from behind her.

She then heard the safety of a gun being removed. Everything was now going downhill.

CHAPTER TEN

Sean stood there with his arms wrapped around the woman Mia saw him hugged up with. He was happy about his success. This shipment will bring in enough money to pay back Tony. If not all, at least half. Maybe he could work something out with him or maybe not. Sean wasn't the begging type and wasn't about to start now. If anything, Tony would be the one begging. Everything was going as planned until he looked up and saw what Angela was staring at. Lil Nicky was holding the woman he is supposed to marry at gunpoint.

"Aye yo boss," Lil Nicky called out. "Look what I found stashed outside the window. Pretty little thing. If you don't want her, I'll have her."

"Sean, tell this asshole to get his hands off me now!" she screamed.

"Let her go," Sean insisted.

"You know this chick?"

"I'm his fiancée, you prick!"

"Oh shit. Didn't know you had a girl," he replied.
Sean was pissed as he walked up to Mia. "What
the fuck are you doing here?" he asked.

"What I am doing here!" she yelled. "What are
you doing here? With this and that?" she said as she
gestured toward everything, including the hostess from the
restaurant. "How could you do this to me? To us?"

"I told you to stay out of this! I got everything
under control."

"You call selling drugs a way out? He was right
about you."

"Who?"

'Who do you think? Don't play dumb Sean. I
thought you were smarter than this." Those were his
words that he said to her earlier.

"So, you've been discussing me with that
asshole?" he argued.

"Well, it looks like you haven't been discussing me
at all," she said as she looked past him to Angela, the
hostess. Mia was ready to swing at her at any minute, but
she knew a low life like Angela wasn't worth it.

"It's not what you think."

"What am I supposed to think? We're supposed
to be getting married, Sean. Married!"

"And we still are. I know this looks bad, but I'm doing this for us. I'm the man in this family, and when I say I will take care of it, trust that I will take care of it," he said as he stared her in the eyes. "You need to leave."

"I'm not leaving until I get some answers," she demanded.

"Do I need to shut this bitch up," Angela stated. She had never seen Mia before until she showed up at Tony's restaurant. She would always hear her name, but Sean made sure to keep Mia's identity a secret. Now Tony wanted her too.

"Bitch? Who are you calling a bitch!" Mia yelled as she leaped at Angela but wasn't fast enough as Sean caught her around her waist.

"Calm down!" both of you.

"Get your hands off me," she said as she pulled away. "I don't know who you are anymore."

"You need to do something, or she will rat you out," said Angela. "I know her type."

"You don't know a damn thing about me. Neither one of you," she said as she stared at Sean.

"Just go home, ok. I'll explain everything later," he said as he grabbed her by the arm and tried to pull her away. She quickly removed herself from his grip.

"Don't touch me with your filthy hands!" she yelled again. Before she knew what was happening, she gave him a backhand across his face. It caught him off guard. She could tell he was even more pissed.

"Leave now or else," he said to her. His demeanor had changed while his rage was beginning to show. He didn't want to look weak in front of his friends. He needed them to see who was in charge and to show them that no one is off-limits. "Nick, see to it that she finds her way out," he said as he began walking away. "Make sure she leaves right away."

"You got it," he said as he went to grab her arm, but she moved out of the way.

She watched him walk away side by side with a now new enemy on her list. She tried her best to hold back the tears because she couldn't let him see that he's gotten the best of her. She knew from the restaurant that the hostess didn't like her and now she knew why.

"Let's go." Lil Nicky said as he walked her to her car, where she got in. He stood there until she drove off.

She drove off and didn't look back. She wanted to cry, but part of her wanted revenge. How did she not see this coming? How did Tony know more about the man she was going to marry than she did? Everything was happening so fast that this was definitely an eye-opener for her. In a short amount of time, her world was turned upside down.

She drove slowly while her mind was in deep thought. She didn't want to go home, at least not right now. She could stay with her friend Kayla, but she just wanted to be alone. She didn't really feel like discussing anything to anyone except for one person.

Her phone buzzed as she continued to drive

slowly. She'd forgotten that she placed it on vibrate earlier, right before she got to the warehouse. She looked at it. She had one voicemail from a number that she didn't recognize. She was curious, so she checked it right away. After hearing the voicemail, she gave a smile. Her night just got even more interesting. She knew it was only a matter of time before she received a phone call demanding her presence.

She was tired of playing the good girl. She was no longer the weak girl she was stronger than this. It was at this point she realized Tony was right. She deserved better than this, but if Sean thought he could get away with this, he was in for a rude awakening. Two could play this game, but only one would win.

CHAPTER ELEVEN

Mia drove her car to the designated location. An upscale grand hotel. She felt a little bad about not going home first to change, but then again, she didn't care. Maybe he would take one look at her and have a change of mind.

She pulled up, and just as she was about to get out, the valet attendant came to her car, stopping her.

"Ms. Lang?" asked the attendant.

"Yes, that's me. Is something wrong?" she asked.

"No ma'am, nothing is wrong. We were instructed to show you to your private parking spot," he said as he pointed to a spot near the front entrance. "It's right over there."

"Oh, ok, thank you," she said shockingly.

"You're welcome, ma'am. Enjoy your stay," he said before waving her off.

Mia didn't know what to think, but she wasn't complaining. She hated parking inside of the dark garages and hated having to wait for her car whenever she got ready to leave. She parked and freshened up her face and switched out her flip flops with her red bottom black heels. She was happy her jacket was long enough to cover most of her gown. She placed a tiny bit of makeup on, but nothing major. A little pop of lip gloss and mascara was all she needed. After all, she wasn't trying to impress anyone anymore.

She fluffed out her hair before getting out of her car. She walked with a forced smile as she was greeted by the attendants. They not only smiled at her but were also checking her out.

"Good evening, ma'am," said one guy as he held open the door for her.

"Good evening," she replied with another forced smile. She could still feel their eyes on her as she walked towards the elevators. "At least someone finds me attractive," she thought to herself.

The doors opened, and she got on. She followed the directions that were left on her voicemail and pressed the twelfth floor. It was the last floor. Her ride up seemed to take forever. Maybe it was because she was nervous. The phone call was from someone else other than Tony. The thoughts of being set up ran through her mind.

"What if this is a setup?" she said to herself as the elevator came to a stop. She hesitated at first before she took her first step off into a short hallway that led to a door. She slowly made her way to the door, and right as she was about to knock, the door opened. She should have been scared, but somehow, she felt relieved.

"What happened? You look like you saw a ghost," Tony said as he held open the door for the most beautiful woman in the world.

"I've just had a long night," she said as he closed the door behind her. For the first time that night, somehow, her smile was real.

"Can I take your jacket?" he asked, but she quickly declined. He was still in his gray dress pants and a white buttoned-down dress shirt that was slightly opened at the top.

"No, thank you." She didn't want him to get the wrong idea if he saw what she was wearing underneath the jacket. Plus, she knew what he was capable of with just a kiss and a touch. After all the lonely nights of being alone, she wasn't sure if being there was a great idea. If he gave her all of him, she might not be able to contain herself.

He stood next to her as his hand found hers. She looked down at it, wondering if she should pull her hand away but decided on keeping it there. The smell of his cologne was so intoxicating that she didn't hear him asking her if she wanted a drink.

"Mia, are you ok?" he asked.

"Um yeah. Sorry…I um I just was thinking about something."

"You care to share with me?" he asked as he stared at her.

"Not really. I don't want to bore you," she said with a smile.

"Well, I'm here if you need to talk. I'm a good listener."

"Thanks."

"Can I get you anything to drink? Beer, wine, champagne, club soda, water or something harder?" he said as he looked her up and down.

She could use something harder. "A glass of wine would do, please." She watched him open a bottle of wine and fill the two glasses that sat on the minibar counter. He handed her one glass as he took the other one.

"Cheers," he said as he held up his glass.

"Cheers," she replied as they tapped their glasses together and took a sip. "So um…you have a lovely place here."

"Thank you. The view overlooks the city. At night its quite lovely, but not as lovely as you," he said as he pulled her close. Her back was facing him as he pressed himself against her. He then draped his arm around her waist as he placed a soft kiss on the side of her neck

She closed her eyes and breathed in the scent of him. She could hear him set his glass down on the minibar. He turned her around and took the glass from her hand and placed it beside his.

He leaned down and kissed her again gently while cupping her face between his hands. He wanted her so badly, but only if she wanted him the same way. He felt no resistance, so he kept going. This time her hands went around his neck, pulling him closer as his hands drifted to her ass. A moan escaped her lips when he traced the outline of her thong and found her treasure.

"We have too many clothes on," he whispered against her lips.

"I agree," she said breathlessly.

He wasted no time removing her jacket and dropped it on the floor. He then helped her unbutton his shirt before it laid crumpled on the floor next to her jacket. She could feel his body through her gown, but she wanted more. They passionately kissed until he lifted her up in his arms. She then wrapped her legs around him as he carried her to his bedroom. He then placed her down on the bed and laid between her legs as they continued kissing. He let his hand drift to her breast before circling the nipple with his fingers. He stopped only for a second to take in the view before him.

"You're beautiful," he said as he stood up and unzipped his pants.

The sound of the zipper had more than Mia's

heart beating. Her clit was throbbing against the seat of her panties, just waiting to be freed. She watched as his pants fell from his waist and then his boxers. She stared at him as she watched him stroke his cock. He was big, and from the looks of it, he knew how to use it. He came closer to reposition himself between her legs. Before she knew what was going to happen, he ripped the gown open and devoured her breast with his lips.

He sucked and licked while his hand slid down inside of her panties and found her jewel. He let his finger go in and out before spreading her juices around her clit. He then kissed her lips hard as he rubbed her until she got wetter and wetter. Just when she was on the edge of exploding, he stopped and sucked his fingers. This sent him over the edge, and now he wanted more. He then ripped her panties on each side so he could get better access. He slid his hands under her ass and lifted her up for full access before letting his tongue go to work.

It's been too long since she was pleasured by a man, so she tried to keep her cool but failed. She moaned and buckled under him as he worked his magic. She knew she was loud but didn't care.

He kissed his way back up, stopping again to feast on her breast before whispering in her ear. "Are you sure this is what you want?" he asked.

"Do I have a choice?" she replied. He was positioned at her entrance, which was making it hard for her to think or say no.

"There's always a choice doll face," he said before

kissing her ever so gently.

"Then, I'm sure. I want you," she said as she whispered against his lips, followed by a gasp as he entered her. She saw that he was big, but he felt bigger. He was rough but gentle as he moved in and out. She held on as he picked up his pace.

He then flipped her over so that she was on top. She rested her hands on his chest as she rode him. She could feel the warm sensation of his mouth on her breast as he teased them, each with his tongue. He ran his fingers through her hair and pulled her down so that they were chest to chest. With one hand around her waist, the other hand slid down her back, where it grazed her asshole. He pumped faster and faster. She could tell he was about to explode, and so was she. Even though she was on top, he still took control. He was a manly man, and it showed. He fucked her harder until they both came. He pulled out and shot his load between her ass cheeks as she rested on his chest.

This was all new to her. She and Sean never lasted this long. She could get used to this, but she already knew he wasn't the keeping type. She started to move off him, but he stopped her.

"Where do you think you are going?" he asked as he looked at her. He was still breathing hard.

"I was going to freshen up and leave. I know how this goes."

"No…. you don't know how this goes. I want you to

stay the night," he said as he pulled her close and kissed her on the forehead.

"Ok." That was all she said as she laid her head back down. She knew tonight moved a little too fast, but she didn't care. Tonight, she wanted to let her hair down. All rules were out the door.

CHAPTER TWELVE

The next morning Tony sat in his club chair smoking a cigar. He stared at the beautiful woman lying in his bed. His eyes followed the curve of her body outlined by the white sheet. He was accustomed to one-night stands, but with this one, he wanted more. He's only known her for a very short time, yet it felt like forever. No woman has had this effect on him like her.

He watched her from a distance but never wanted to intrude on another man's property. Growing up, he didn't have the happiest home. He saw his father cheat on his mother with tons of women. Doing so caused his mother a great amount of pain. He vowed never to cause that pain to any woman, so he stayed unattached. That was until he saw Mia. He watched Sean with her and realized he didn't deserve her. He would often brag about Mia, but still, she wasn't enough. His innocent flirting with other women caused him to cheat multiple times. Tony often wondered if Mia knew anything about it. Something still puzzled him. Why did she not resist him? He didn't take her for the cheating kind, but either way, she was going to be his.

Watching her body move beneath the sheets was waking up a part of his body that didn't need to be woken up. He had things to do, places to go, and people to see, with Sean being the main hit on his list. He needed to show him that he fucked with the wrong man. No one steals from him and gets away with it. Letting him walk free would send the wrong kind of message, and before you know it, every fucker would try him. His thoughts were interrupted when he saw her staring at him.

"Good morning," she said as she stared at him. Her view of him was clear as he sat with his boxers on. His body was amazingly built. Her eyes drifted below. She smiled when she thought of last night. He was more than she could handle, but she loved a challenge.

"Good morning," he said as he puffed on his cigar.

"Started early, I see."

He gave one big puff before putting it out. "Don't worry. If you don't like it, I won't smoke it around you."

Mia sat up in bed as her mind fell back on last night's episode at the warehouse. She loved Sean, but her love for him became tarnished. She should feel bad for ending up in bed with his enemy, but she didn't. Everything happens for a reason. She wondered if the man sitting before her was that reason.

"Come here," he said. He had meetings to attend, but it needed to wait. He had more important things to tend to right now.

Mia said nothing as she got up from the bed. She kept the sheet draped in front of her to hide her goodness from him. Even after last night's heated session, she still felt somewhat shy.

Tony stared her in the eyes as he tossed the sheet aside. "You're perfect, no need to hide from me," he said as he took in her beauty before him. He then grabbed her around the waist and pulled her close, causing her to straddle him. He wasted no time removing his shorts.

She should leave, but desire took over when she felt his thick rod brushing against her entrance. She was already wet and waiting for him. With one try, he pushed and slipped in. He buried his face in her breasts as she rode him fast and hard. She closed her eyes and worked her hips. He was deep inside of her.

"Fuck!" he grunted as he grabbed her by the hips. He pounded her harder and harder until he couldn't last any longer. He pulled out just in time and spilled his seed against her wetness. He grunted until he was completely emptied. He pulled her close and kissed her hard. "One day, there won't be any pulling out," he whispered against her lips.

Mia didn't know what to say. What did that even mean? One thing for sure, she was glad the doorbell rang.

"Your doorbell is ringing," she said with a smile. "You mind if I shower?"

"No. If you need anything, just let me know. I can have whatever you need to be delivered to you."

"Thanks," she replied as she eased off him. She walked with her legs closed together until she was inside the bathroom.

Tony followed Mia into the bathroom to a separate vanity, where he quickly wiped himself off before throwing on a shirt and a pair of sweatpants.

"I'm coming! I'm coming! This better be fucking good!" he yelled as he made his way to the door. He glanced through the peephole before opening it. It was his underboss Sal and one of his associates named Nicholas Featherstone, but those who know him called him Lil Nicky. He opened the door and greeted them as usual.

"Took you fucking long enough to answer the door. Remind me to get you a fucking scooter," Sal joked as they both laughed.

Sal was like a brother to him. They grew up next door together and went to school together. By the time they were eighteen and out of school, they both decided to go their separate ways. Sal moved to upstate New York while Tony moved to Chicago. Even though they were miles away, they never lost touch. Over the years, they've learned from each other, which brought them back to their hometown, Memphis.

"Nice place you have here," said Lil Nicky as his eyes roamed the place. It was his first time there. "You must bring all the chicks here?" He laughed as he pointed towards Mia's shoe and a pile of clothing on the floor.

No one laughed as they stared at Featherstone. "What's with this kid?" said Tony. "You taught him the ropes yet?"

"I'm teaching him all the things you taught me and more, but he's a hothead. Doesn't know when to shut the fuck up," Sal stated.

"I'm not that bad, sir," Lil Nicky said to Tony. Your boy here just takes things too seriously."

"This is serious. You think what we do here is a fucking game?" Tony said furiously.

"No, sir," said Lil Nicky as he held up both hands.

"If you want to hang with the best, you need to think like the best, act like the best, and dress like the best." Tony looked Lil Nicky up and down. He was displeased with how he was dressed. Normally he could care less of how his employees dressed, but he was dressed like a bum. "What are you two doing here anyway?"

"Another truck was seized last night," said Sal.

"Shit! What about the merchandise?"

"Everything was seized. All the imported goods too. They found drugs on it. Ever since the first bust, the feds have made sure to keep a close eye on all shipments."

Tony said nothing as he sat in deep thought. He just couldn't wrap his mind around drugs being on his shipments. Someone was behind it, and he planned on making sure every person was dealt with accordingly.

"Who was the driver?" Tony asked.

"Jimmy, I believe was the driver," said Sal. "I questioned him as soon as he called me. He didn't see anyone or anything unusual when he went to pick up the load."

Jim Greene is also known as Jimmy Boy, only worked for Tony for a few years. He was another friend of the family that he learned to trust over the years, but trusting him didn't come easy. Jim had to prove that he was willing to risk it all, including death if that time ever came. He proved to Tony with little to no effort that he was the man to have on his team. A ceremony was held, swearing Jimmy into the well-known mafioso family where he served his training under Tony's lifelong friend Sal.

"Somebody is behind this. They're trying to fuck with me. Don't they know who I am by now? Don't they know the connections that I have? I can't be touched!" he yelled. He was beyond furious. With every tampered shipment comes a loss of profit. He didn't believe in being wasteful, especially with money.

"You mind if I have a drink?" asked Lil Nicky, but no one said a word. "Ok, I'll take that as a yes." He smiled and walked towards the bar and began fixing himself a drink while leaving the two of them to finish talking business.

"Whoever is behind this, we will catch them. It's only a matter of time before there's a fuck up," said Sal. "We will start with Sean."

They were so deep in their conversation that they didn't hear Mia's footsteps as she entered the room.

"Is everything ok?" Mia said as she stood with a white robe on, a robe that belonged to Tony. It fit her body loosely as it hung to the floor. She had her arms wrapped around her body, making sure to keep it closed. She didn't need anything falling out. "I thought her I heard you yelling."

"Everything is ok," Tony said as he went to stand in front of Mia. He placed both hands on the side of her face and pulled her close. He then placed a tender kiss upon her lips.

"Sorry to bother you," she whispered.

"No bother, sweetheart," he replied as he slid his arm around her. "You remember Sal on your first meeting?"

"Hi again," she said as she waved.

"If you have any problems and can't reach me, you contact Sal. He'll get the job done," he said with great pride.

"Well, that's always good to know," she replied. "Who's that over there?" She pointed to Lil Nicky as he sat at the bar with his back facing everyone.

"That right there, he's a nobody, a fucking loser with

a big mouth," Tony stated.

He took the last drink from his glass before turning around. "Who are you fucking calling a loser?" Lil Nicky said with anger as he got up from the chair. He became quiet as he saw Mia standing there.

Mia couldn't say a word as she stepped back. The minute she saw his face, she recognized him. "I um......I need to go," she stated as she quickly grabbed her things from the floor. She headed straight towards the bedroom to get dressed.

Tony sensed something was wrong and followed her. "What's wrong? You look like you saw a ghost."

"Nothing is wrong. I just need to go. I'm supposed to go into work for a few hours."

He pulled her close into his arms. He wanted her to know that whatever it was, he would protect her. "What's wrong?" He asked again softly.

Mia looked him in the eyes and wondered how someone like him could be so masculine yet be so gentle? The way he looked at her made her want to trust him, and she did.

"I saw him before," she replied.

"What do you mean you saw him before?"

"I saw him last night before coming here."

"Doll face, you're losing me here. What's going on?"

Tony said as he stared at her. "You seeing him too?"

"No! Gosh no. Nothing like that." She hesitated a little before telling him the entire story. She didn't want him to think what happened between them was out of pity. "I'm sorry I didn't tell you before."

"It's ok," he said before kissing her. He wanted more, but now just wasn't the time. "You've helped me out more than you would ever know."

"How so? I know I should have told you before. I just wanted to forget last night."

"I now know that I have more than one rat to deal with. I knew I hated that kid from the moment I saw him."

"What are you going to do?" She was concerned. She didn't want to be the reason anyone was killed. She knew his kind too well. A sit down for a nice conversation never ends well.

"Don't worry. Just carry on with your day. I will check on you later, but if you need me sooner, you know how to reach me." He kissed her again and gave her ass a squeeze before turning to leave.

Mia watched him walk away and smiled. She didn't know if meeting him was a mistake or a perfect mistake.

"One more thing, you're off the market. Even to that scum bag of yours," he said before closing the door. He returned to the living room to see Sal standing alone. "Where is the little fucker?" was all Tony said.

CHAPTER THIRTEEN

Mia was happy the lobby area at his penthouse was semi-empty. She didn't need anyone staring at the sight of her clothes, which were torn from Tony's aggressiveness from last night's lovemaking. Even though her jacket covered her, she thought she looked suspicious, holding it so close to her body. She sped home and quickly searched for something to wear before leaving out for work. Four hours later, Mia sat at her desk, bothered by the thought of everything that was going on. She wasn't a snitch, but she felt the need to tell Tony about her findings with Sean. Everyone thought highly of him, but they also feared him. She heard many stories in the past about him. Maybe they never saw the side of him that she saw. The side of him that was gentle and seemed to care wholeheartedly.

Her mind then wandered on the guy that she saw at Tony's. She had no idea that he was working for Sean and Tony too. A stupid move on his part, but an even deadlier move for working for Tony. A young guy like him should be making the best out of his life instead of dealing with drugs.

She glanced up at the clock on the wall as time seemed to tick away slowly. She then checked her phone for any new messages. There were only missed calls displayed from Sean asking her to call him, followed by dozens of text messages. He wasn't at home anyway this morning when she arrived. Which she was happy because she didn't have the strength to argue. She didn't feel the need to contact him, so she just hit the ignore button on her phone. After the stunt he pulled, the wedding was officially off. How could she marry someone that kept her in the dark and someone she could no longer trust? What good was a marriage if the trust was broken? Just the thought of it reminded her of her parents. Her father broke the trust, and for years, her parents struggled to rebuild what took a lifetime to make and a second to break. She saw the hurt it caused her mother and couldn't imagine living her life like that.

She held her phone up and stared at the background. It was a photo of Sean and her that was taken months ago on a night out. Bittersweet memories flushed down the drain as she replaced the photo with one of herself. Moving on would be easy and for the best. Even though it wasn't what she wanted, it was what she needed. When she loves, she loves hard. But once you do her wrong, she was over you and through. Life was too short. Plus, she had someone else to deal with now. Once the debt was paid in full, she was leaving town.

Her phone rang, almost causing her to drop it on the floor. An unexpected call that she probably shouldn't answer, but she did anyway.

"Hello?" she answered softly.

"Hello, gorgeous," Tony replied.

"Hi, Tony."

"How's your day so far?" he asked. This was all new for him, calling a woman to ask how her day was had never happened before. After sex, he would make them leave the same night. He never had a woman to spend the night. If his love or feelings was not involved, they had to leave. He would let them all know from the beginning that it was a fuck fest and not a sleepover. Never expect anything from him afterward. Not even a hug, but with Mia, it was different. She gave him butterflies. She made him feel something that he's never felt before.

"My day is going ok, I guess."

"You guess? Why you guess?"

"So much is happening."

"So much like what?"

She waited a few seconds before saying anything. She needed to make sure she said the right thing. "Everything with Sean and the money. Time is winding down, and I still don't know if he will have the money."

"Don't worry your pretty little head. Everything will work out fine at the end. You'll see."

"What are you going to do to him?" Even though Sean pissed her off, she still didn't want anything bad to happen to him. They had a history together, and unfortunately, now they were history.

"Don't worry about that. Just worry about having dinner with me tonight."

She didn't have plans and damn near didn't have a choice. She wasn't ready to face Sean yet. He was probably somewhere banging that hostess lady anyway.

"Sure, where bout?" she asked.

"I'll let you know the address later," he replied. He was smitten by Mia but wasn't a damn fool. Tonight, he wanted to know more about her. He wanted to know the things that no one else knew. He wanted to know all of her.

"Ok. I guess I will wait for your call. Well, I really should get back to work. Oh, and one more thing I was wondering, what happened to the guy that was in the room?" she asked nervously.

"Don't worry about him. He won't bother you."

"I'm not really worried about that. I......I just didn't want you to hurt him." She knew she was overstepping her boundaries by questioning him, but she wanted a piece of mind that the guy was ok.

"I told you don't worry about him. He's ok."

For the first time that day, she smiled. A dead body because of her was now off her mind. She could have a clear conscience to finish up her work.

"Look doll face, I gotta go. Just make sure you show up. Ok?"

"Ok," she replied before she heard the dial tone. She thought about tonight and Sean again. She needed to call him back, but she already knew how the conversation would go. If he found out that she slept with his rival, he would be furious, but she needed to call him. She wanted to make sure he was ok.

She picked up the phone and made the phone call to him. Ever since shit hit the fan, they barely spoke. The phone rang once before it was answered.

"Mia," said Sean as he answered the phone.

"Hi Sean," she replied.

"Where are you? I waited up for you to come home last night."

Mia remembered those days where she would wait up for him. Now the tables have turned. "I was out."

"Out? Out with him?" he asked. The thought of her being with him boiled his blood.

"Can we not do this right now? I was only returning your calls. What do you want?"

"I want you to come home so we can work things out."

"What's to work out? You've been lying the entire time to me. Every time I asked you to talk to me and tell me what's going on, you lied. Now you want to talk about it?" A knock on her door interrupted their conversation. It was a well-needed interruption. "I have to go, Sean," she replied as she hung up. "Come in."

"Hey Mia, sorry to bother you, but there's a lady asking for you," said Terri. She was a clerk that worked at the front desk, along with several other employees. Mia once worked the front desk as well but was promoted a few months ago.

"Another unsatisfied crazy customer?" Mia joked.

"Oh, no. I don't think she's a customer. Well, I've never seen her around. At least not on this shift. She demanded to see you or else. I just wanted to tell you in person. You might want to take your earrings off for this."

"It's probably just some customer wanting a refund for receiving late room services or not enough towels," Mia thought to herself as she got up from her desk. "Let's see what all the noise is about."

As she stepped out of her office, she could hear the loudness coming from the front area. A loud voice of a woman demanding to speak to Mia ASAP! She followed Terri down the short hall until she rounded the corner. Terri was right. She should have taken her earrings off for this one.

It was Angela the hostess demanding to speak with her and carrying on a scene in front of the customers. Mia knew better not to get close to her. She stayed behind the counter, where she felt a little safe. She needed to get her off the premises fast before she runs away customers. They were a high-class hotel and didn't need any publicity.

"You bitch, you fucking little bitch!" Angela yelled as she saw Mia.

"You need to leave," Mia stated as she tried to remain professional.

"I'm not leaving until you tell me, what did you do? What did you do!" she yelled again.

Mia was confused about what was being asked. She barely knew her, and now she was at her job, causing a scene. "What are you talking about!"

"What did you do? Did you bribe him with your looks to make him hurt my baby? You're nothing but a snitch!" she said as she continued to yell.

"Look, I haven't the slightest idea of what you are talking about. Why don't you just leave before security throws you out."

"You know damn well what I am talking about. Your new man almost killed my son Nicky. After he saw you there at his whore house, Tony made sure that he would keep his mouth shut. He beat my baby until he was unconscious and dropped him off at my doorstep! All because of you!" Angela screamed as she launched at Mia.

Mia jumped back. Angela was crazy and obviously high on something. "I don't know what you are talking about. Where is security? Someone, call security now!" she yelled. "You need to leave!"

Angela looked around to see security coming towards her, but it didn't stop her from telling Mia how she felt. "You're nothing to him. He'll use you, just like he used me. Your promotion and everything else will be taken away once he's finished with you. Then we'll see who'll have the last laugh," she said before security grabbed her by the arm. She furiously snatched her arm away then left, leaving Mia with an ear full.

Her day just got interesting. Was this job part of his plan? Every day she came into work and gave her best. Now, she just found out everything that she worked hard for was a lie. He's been trailing her for a while, and she wanted to know why, but first, she needed to make a stop.

CHAPTER FOURTEEN

Tony sat in his home office, watching the security monitor as Mia's car drove up. He had been waiting for her all day. Her touch, her smell, and the feel of her body he craved like water on a hot day in a desert. After a few minutes, he watched her as she exited her vehicle. She wore a short black long sleeve dress with an open back. Her simple black strappy heels made her legs appear longer. He smiled at the thought of them wrapped around his waist. He was so mesmerized that he didn't hear the doorbell ring.

Normally he would have a small staff there, but they were all gone for the night, except for the cook. He made his way to the door, dressed in black dress pants and a white shirt. Even though they were at his private home, he wanted the night to be special. He wanted to get to know her on another level.

The doorbell rang for a second time before he opened the door. Standing before him was a gift he'd been waiting to unwrap. "I'm glad you decided to come," he said as he took her by the hand and escorted her inside.

"Did I have a choice?" she asked sarcastically.

"You always have a choice," he replied. "You look beautiful tonight."

"Thank you," she said as she turned towards him. "You don't look bad yourself." She held her head down shyly as she complimented him.

He placed a hand under her chin and lifted her face. He wanted to look in her brown eyes before he showed her just how much he missed her. He placed a tender kiss upon her lips, leaving them both wanting more. He then placed both hands around her as she placed her hands around his neck. Their lips interlocked again, leaving no room for air.

She could feel just how bad he wanted her by the bulge that pressed against the front of his pants. She needed to focus on way more important things, at least for now. She pulled away slowly, giving them a little space between them. She needed to catch her breath so that she could say what she really needed to say.

"So, I um...... I got a visitor today at my job."

"Oh yeah, what did he want?"

"It wasn't a he. It was more like a she. Angela. Your hostess."

"Ugh. What did she want?" he asked as he wrapped his arms around her again.

"She wanted me to know what exactly happened to

her son," she said as she stepped away from him. She needed more space between them. Standing so close caused her to lose sight of her thoughts and caused parts of her to awaken as if they had a mind of their own. "She told me her son was beaten and left at her doorstep. At first, I had no idea what or who she was talking about, but as she kept talking…I figured it out. You told me you wouldn't hurt him."

Tony hated being questioned, but he knew she was only being concerned. He trusted her, but he knew he still had to be cautious. She had the heart that he could never have, a heart that could never hurt anyone or at least not on purpose. She thought with her heart, while he thought with his head. In his world, he had to be emotionless. He had to show no fear, or others would find him weak and powerless.

"He was fine the last I've seen of him. I mean……he had a few cuts and bruises but nothing serious."

Mia stood there with her arms crossed while she stared at him. It didn't take a rocket scientist to read between the lines. She knew exactly what he was talking about, but she knew he would never admit to it. They never do.

"She thinks I am the reason why. Now I have a crazy person that might try something stupid. I need to watch my back now. I don't trust her."

"And you shouldn't. I've known her for a while. We should have dinner before it gets cold," he said as he quickly changed the subject. He placed his arm around her waist and guided her to a room he had prepared, especially for her.

"It's beautiful," said Mia.

"I hoped that you would like it."

"I...I love it." Her eyes roamed the room. The table was set for two and was tastefully decorated as the shadows of the candlelight danced against the wall. Her eyes then lingered on the set of closed doors. "May I," she asked.

"Sure," he replied with a smile.

She walked slowly towards the doors and opened them, revealing the city lights from a distance. She turned towards him and gave a little smile before focusing back on the beauty before her. The breeze softly hit her face as soon as she walked out. She leaned against the railing taking in the peacefulness that surrounded her.

Tony stood back and watched her from behind. The outline of her body in her black dress revealed every curve that he couldn't wait to explore. The open back of her dress screamed for his attention, and he did just that. He walked up to her from behind and placed a kiss on her upper back before placing a kiss on her neck. He wanted her now but wanted to take it slow. The night was still young.

"It's so peaceful out here. You're close to the city, but far enough to have......this," she said as she gestured towards the city lights. She was so at peace that she didn't realize she was embracing his embrace. Her mind totally had forgotten everything that was going on in her life. If only this was forever.

"I can show you around later, there's another balcony with even better views, but first about we have dinner," he whispered in her ear.

"Yeah, we should," she stated as she turned around.

He placed his hand at the crease of her back and led her back inside, where he held out the chair for her.

"Thank you," she said.

"You're welcome," he stated as he took a seat. "Wine?"

"Sure, but not too much."

He popped open the bottle of wine and began pouring into each glass until they were half full.

"There you go. The cook will be out shortly."

She slowly took a sip of her red wine. She hoped that it would help loosen her up a bit. "You have a cook? Why am I not surprised?"

"What? You don't think I can cook?"

"I'm not saying that. You just don't seem like the cooking type. Too dapper for that."

"You're right, I'm not the best, but I can do a hell of a job eating," he said as he stared at her.

She smiled shyly and changed the subject. "So, um, tell me about yourself?" She wanted to bring up her job promotion but went against it. She didn't want to ruin the night since he went out of his way to make it special.

"What do you want to know?"

"Anything. Your background. How did you become who you are?"

He smiled and gave a chuckle. His background was complex. Many didn't understand why he was the way he was. Even after explaining it, they still didn't get it. They will never get it.

He grew up with his two brothers Carmine and Frankie. His father was Irish, and his mother was Italian. At an early age, they all learned the family business, a trading business his father inherited from his grandfather. By the time they were older, things had changed. The business changed, and more importantly, their family changed. The Feds eventually convicted his father and some of his crewmates on extortion and racketeering. This led to him and his brothers taking over the business. Their mother didn't want them to end up like their father, so they did things differently. Even though they did things differently, they still maintain the strength and power behind the family name. The family was always first. Until this day, most fear them, while the others wanted to join them.

Mia stared at him as he told her about himself. She was surprised that he told her as much as he did. She began to see a different side of him that she didn't think existed.

"This family business, can you just do an early retirement and find something else to do?" she asked.

"There is no retiring," he said as he laughed. "This is all I know. This is part of me."

They both looked around to see the cook coming through the door. An older guy by the name of Melvin, who was also the cook. He was a close family friend that's been more like an uncle to Tony.

"Mia, I want to you meet Uncle Melvin, the best cook there is," said Tony.

"Hi, nice to meet you," she said shyly as she watched him place both plates down in front of them.

"The pleasure is all mine," Melvin stated. "You take good care of my boy here. He's like a son to me."

"I'll do my best," she said as she smiled. She couldn't help but notice the smirk on Tony's face. "Everything looks and smells delicious."

"Uncle Melvin, what are we having?" Tony interrupted.

"Your mother's favorite. Melanzane alla parmigiana and for dessert cassata siciliana," Melvin stated.

"Similar to chicken parmesan, but with eggplant and for dessert, something similar to a cheesecake," said Tony. He knew Mia had no idea of what he was talking about.

"I'm sure it tastes as good as it looks," she replied. She was hungry and couldn't wait to dig in.

"Well, I'll leave you kids to enjoy," said Melvin before turning to leave.

"More wine?" asked Tony.

Mia looked down at her glass and noticed that it was almost empty. "Yes, please," she replied. "I guess I needed it more than I thought."

"You and me both," he smiled.

They both sat, ate, and enjoyed each other's company. They both laughed and talked about their childhood. She was having fun. Maybe a little too much fun being in his presence. He made her feel special while she made him feel complete.

Hours had passed before she noticed the time. "It's getting late. I should probably get going," she said as she pushed her chair back from the table. Things didn't go as planned, but she wondered if tonight was the start of something new. Only time would tell.

Tony joined her as she stood up from the table. "Maybe you should stay a little longer," he said as he stood beside her.

"I really can't. I have to be at work super early."

"How about I show you around. I still owe you that amazing view."

She wanted to say no, but how could she deny the man that held her and Sean's life in his hand. "Ok," she replied.

Tony and Mia made their way upstairs towards another room. He gave her a brief history of the house along the way until they reached their destination. It was a sitting area, furnished with all white furnishing, floor to ceiling windows, and another amazing skyline of the city. Tony wasted no time opening the doors to the balcony. Mia followed him as he stepped outside. The balcony was a little larger in size. A small table and two chairs were in the corner as well as a large tufted chaise lounge.

"Wow! You weren't kidding about the view. It's definitely amazing!" She said as she felt his arms go around her waist.

The night air gave her a slight chill as he pulled her closer. Once again, she embraced his warmth. She closed her eyes and could feel the tiny kisses he placed on her shoulder and neck. He kept one hand around her waist while the other traveled through the opening of the back of her dress. He didn't stop until he reached the fullness of her breast and began taunting the nipple until it was hard under his touch. He was happy she wasn't wearing a bra.

Again, she wanted to say no and pull away, but she was wrapped under the spell of his touch. He had a way with his hands that made her want him more. She was beginning to understand why all the women wanted him. Her body began to yearn more as his other hand found its way to her other nipple. His kisses and touch together were a dangerous pair. She pushed back against him. This time he removed both of his hands and pulled the top down to her waist. He then turned her around and took them each into his mouth. He dabbled his tongue around her nipples, taking turns to make sure neither one was left untouched.

Her arms went around his neck, all while pulling him as close as he could go. She wanted more and needed more, and more was what she got. He lifted her off her feet as he carried her over to the chaise lounge chair and positioned her on both knees. He then raised her dress up, scrunching it around her waist so that he could have full access to her round ass. He planted a tender kiss on each cheek before sliding her panties aside. He wanted a full view. He had dessert earlier, but it was nothing compared to what he was going to taste right now.

Mia was in pure ecstasy as she felt the touch of his lips. He began kissing his way until he reached her jewel. The more he found her rhythm, the more she began bucking against his tongue. When she knew he was finished, he would come back for more, diving his tongue in and out of her as he licked and sucked. Her knees were weak, and she was almost ready to throw in the white flag until he slowed up. Then just when she thought she couldn't take anymore, the sound of his zipper prepared her for what was to come.

CHAPTER FIFTEEN

Sean laid in bed, staring up at the ceiling. He tried calling Mia several times, but each time it went to her voicemail. He regretted doing things the way he did, and if he could start over, he would. His mind began playing memories of the first day they met until it landed on a certain day, the proposal. He knew that he was taking a chance of losing her by not telling her. Now the one thing he never wanted to lose was slipping from his grasp.

"Hey babe," Angela said as she came from the bathroom wearing only her bra and panties. "You ready for round two?"

"No, I should leave. I need to be home with my girl. She doesn't need to know I was here." He gave her that look, reminding her to keep her mouth shut.

Angela couldn't help but laugh and pretended to zip her mouth shut. "Your girl?" she laughed again. "If you think she is still your girl, you are crazier than I thought."

"What is that supposed to mean?"

"She isn't your girl, sweetheart. How clearer can I be?" She reached down onto the floor and pulled out a cigarette from her pants pocket and began to light it. "At least not anymore," she said as she took a puff. "Your girl has a new man. I'm sure you know who."

"Mia wouldn't do that to me. She loves me."

"Hopefully, she doesn't love you the same way you love her," she said as she looked towards the messy bed.

"Whatever. Just keep your mouth shut. We never happen."

Angela rolled her eyes. He wouldn't know love if it bit him in the ass. "If you say so. I know the bitch better watch her back."

"Don't you dare fucking call her that, and you better not lay a hand on her!" he yelled as he sat on the edge of the bed.

Angela was a little taken off guard. He's never yelled at her before. What was it about this Mia person that had two men that she wanted to be wrapped around her finger? Just the thought of her made Angela even madder. She wanted her out of her life and out of the picture. Sean was so in love with Mia, Angela knew he would never belong to her, but she will try her best to make him change his mind. Sean had the drugs while Tony had money and fame. She needed to win them both over.

"You know she's probably somewhere laying up with Tony. Whatever Tony wants, Tony gets, and he got her."

"Shut up!" he yelled. "Keep her name out of your mouth."

"Do you know she snitched on us? She's the reason why my son was beaten," Angela said as she leaned against the dresser, puffing on her cigarette angrily.

"I told you, Mia isn't a snitch!"

"What makes you so sure? You can't even keep her on a leash." She was testing him. She wanted to see how far she could bend him before he breaks.

"Watch your fucking mouth!" Sean yelled.

"Where is she now? Huh?" She questioned as she went to stand in front of him. "You've called her how many times now and still no word from her. She's out fucking him while snitching."

"I told you, keep her name out of your mouth! You don't know what you are talking about," Sean said as he swiped his hands down his face. Everything was beginning to be a little too much for him. "Mia isn't none of those things. She's not like you! She's different, and that's why I love her." His temper was beginning to boil. The thought of that scumbag touching his woman made him want to put a bullet in him.

"You don't know a damn thing about love, sweetheart."

"Go fuck yourself."

"My baby told me that Tony wanted to know who

was behind the seizing of his shipments and because he wouldn't tell…they beat him. They beat my baby all because of her!" She yelled, causing Sean to grip her by the neck while pushing her against the wall. "Get your hands off of me!" She fought to get his hands from around her neck, but he was too strong.

"You work for me, and I am your supplier. Keep the lies up, and I will end all deals with you," he said as he released his grip.

She began coughing as she tried to catch her breath. "If Tony finds out I'm working for both of you, he will kill me. He already tried to kill Nicky. He's a powerful man Sean. Nobody fucks with him and lives to tell the story," she said nervously.

"Nobody fucks with me either," he said as he began putting on clothes.

Angela watched him as he dressed. Sean was smart and handsome, but he was no match for Tony. Tony was born into this type of world while Sean was still learning the ropes.

"We should move away. We could start over together. Maybe a house on the beach. I always wanted that," she said out of the blue. She wanted to see exactly where she stood in his life. She wanted to know if they had a chance.

"I told you, I love Mia. Just continue to play your role and do your job."

"I want more."

Sean said nothing as he looked at her and laughed. She knew that laugh way too well. The same laugh Nicky's dad gave her when she told him she was pregnant. She puffed the last of her cigarette before putting it out. She knew what she had to do. She had a few things up her sleeve. She wasn't the smartest growing up, but she learned a few things in life along the way. One was to always look after yourself because no one else will.

She waited until he was finished dressing before she walked up to him and placed both hands on the side of his face. She wanted to look into his eyes and say what she had to say.

"You know what Sean, you're a good man, but I think it's time we went our separate ways."

"What? I own you until these last shipments have cleared," he stated.

"No, you don't, Sean. You see, that's the problem.........there are no more shipments," she said as she quickly pulled a syringe out of her bra and stabbed it into the side of his neck. "We could have been perfect together."

Sean grabbed his neck and pulled the syringe out. He glanced at it before tossing it on the floor with great surprise. "You trying to kill me, bitch!" he yelled before launching at her.

The deadly look he gave her made Angela wonder if she had given him enough. He wasn't going down as fast as she thought. She ran to get the tossed syringe and stabbed him again. This time she made sure that all of it went in. He then began staggering until he stumbled back onto the bed, where he laid motionless before closing his eyes.

Angela then began rummaging through his pockets in search of any packages that contained drugs. "Where are they!" she yelled, "Fuck." She checked his duffle bag and the pockets and still no sign of drugs. Just a load of cash, he had to stash away later. She was desperate and needed a quick hit but was out of luck. She hurried and got dressed. It was only a matter of time before things got worse.

She walked over to Sean, laying on the bed and straddled him. "I wish things could have ended differently for us Sean, but I'm tired of playing second fiddle," she said as she kissed him on the lips. The sound of doors being opened and closed made her jumped off him. She ran and peeped out of the window. "Looks like we have company."

She puffed another cigarette as she waited by the bedroom window. She looked over at Sean and began to feel a little remorse for what she had done. Their history was strictly business. Somewhere along the way, she developed feelings. She hoped that after being intimate, he would develop some type of feelings too.

Her thoughts were interrupted by footsteps in the hallway. "In here!" she called out.

The door opened, and there stood two of Tony's men Sal and longtime capo Richard Nee, who goes by Rich. With their guns drawn, they began immediately searching the room.

"There's no one else here. I'm alone," said Angela. "I did just like I was told. He's out cold."

"Where's the money?" Richard asked.

"Over there in the bag," she said as she pointed to the duffle bag. "I didn't count it, so I don't know how much it is."

"Who else is involved?" Sal asked as he and Rich counted the money. "He's short?" He then looked up at Angela.

"What? I swear I didn't touch anything," she said nervously.

She hoped Sal would come alone, but she should have known. Richard made her nervous. Any time he was around, nothing good ever happened. People came up missing or dead.

Sal went around the room, recovering little devices tucked away out of plain sight. Rich kept his eyes on Angela as she kept her eyes on them. "Last one," said Sal as he picked her home phone and removed a tiny device.

"What's going on?" Angela asked. "You fucking bugged my place and my phone?"

"I hate liars, Angie," said Rich as he took out a syringe.

Angela stared at the syringe. It was the same drug

she'd given Sean minutes before. She didn't know what was in it. She just knew she didn't want it. "He made me do it. I wouldn't dare betray Tony like that!" she yelled. "You know me!" She wanted to run, but she had nowhere to run. She was cornered in her bedroom. Angela began throwing whatever she could at them as Sal launched at her. He gripped her by the waist as she kicked and screamed. She wasn't going down without a fight.

"This will only hurt a little," said Rich as he stabbed her in the neck. She was small, so it didn't take much. "That wasn't too bad, was it?"

Angela wanted to give Rich a piece of her mind, but she felt her eyes getting heavy as she slowly began losing consciousness. The tears ran down her cheek as he fought to stay awake.

Sal released his grip and threw her over his shoulder. Before they reached the car, she was out.

CHAPTER SIXTEEN

It was late at night when Mia woke up in bed, Tony's bed. The sound of his voice drifted from behind the closed doors connected to the bedroom. She laid there for a few minutes and thought about their escapade earlier. She smiled. Being with him was different, but in a good way. His exterior was hard, oh so hard, but his heart was gentle and soft. At least when it came to her.

Her thoughts faded away as Tony's voice became louder from the other room. She removed the sheet that covered her body and searched for something to put on. Her eyes landed on his white long-sleeved collared shirt laying on a chair. It was big on her, but it worked perfectly. She rolled the sleeves up as she walked towards the door. She carefully placed her ear against it. Whomever he was talking to had him furious.

Tony yelled at the top of his lungs in anger. "I want every fucker that's behind this. This is the third shipment that has been tampered with, and now you're telling me the Feds want to investigate me!"

Tony's rants went on and on as Mia continued to listen behind the door. She came in on the back end to know just what he was talking about. All she knew was that he was now in trouble, and from the sound of it, Sean must be behind it.

"I don't care who it is. You fuck him up, and you fuck him up good. I'll deal with the others once I get there. No, don't whack him. I don't want to deal with the Misses."

After hearing those words, she knew she needed to do something, but what could she do? She needed to keep her cool for when he got off the phone. She didn't want him to know that she overheard his conversation on the phone. Just when she was about to walk away, she heard him call her by the nickname he gave her.

"You can come in doll face," said Tony from behind the closed doors. "

Mia froze in her footsteps. "Shit," she whispered to herself. Her heart began to pound. She had to calm down and get her story together. Now she had to pretend that she didn't hear much, but Tony was smart. He knew bullshit when he smelled it. Plus, she wasn't good at lying. She placed her hands nervously on the door handles and slowly opened the doubled doors. She stood there in his shirt that she forgot that she was wearing as he stared at her.

"Close the door behind you," he demanded as he continued his conversation on the phone. "I'll call you when I'm on the way." He then hung up the phone as he continued staring at Mia in silence.

His stare was making her nervous, that she began fidgeting with her fingers. She didn't know what he was going to say or do next. "I um……I couldn't sleep," she stated, but Tony said nothing. He just continued to stare.

"You know, that shirt looks way better on you than on me," he said. "You make everything look better, even me."

Mia gave a slight smile at his last comment. Her body began to relax and respond to the gentleness that she was familiar with. "How did you know I was there?"

"Your shadow underneath the door gave you away."

"I'm sorry. I wasn't trying to be nosey," she stated as he moved closer. "The sound of your voice woke me up. I wanted to make sure everything was ok, but I didn't want to bother you." She took a deep breath. She was beginning to jumble her words. "I'm so sorry."

"Don't be. There's nothing to be sorry about," he said as he got up from his desk. He slowly walked around it and leaned against the front of it. "Come here."

Mia did as she was told and wasted no time in doing so. He pulled her close and kissed her slowly. A kiss that she seemed to be craving more and more lately. As they opened their eyes and they stared at each other, they both knew something was there. For Mia, it was a sense of feeling wanted. Even though she knew this was going to be temporary. For Tony, it was the first time a woman could make him let his guard down and love. When he looked in her eyes, he saw a woman that he could love. A woman that he could grow his dynasty with and maybe one day become Mrs. Spillane. What was he thinking? A girl like her would never love him or, better yet, choose him. She was nice and timid while he was rough and ruthless.

He pulled her even closer and placed both hands on each side of her face before sliding one hand around her waist. He wanted her to feel what he was going to tell her and not run away. "You are the most beautiful woman in the world to me. I was lucky enough to have you in my presence, but I think it's time you leave."

Mia was confused. "What are you saying?" She questioned.

"Tonight is our last time seeing each other."

"What about the deal? What about the money? I don't know if Sean has all the money?" She asked nervously. She just knew what would happen if she walked out the door. He'll probably riddle her body with bullets or do her execution-style like they do in the movies. "What will happen to me?" Her voice began to crack as she held back the tears. Was this the end for her?

Tony kissed the top of her forehead to soothe her. He hated to see a woman cry, especially her. "Don't cry. You don't have anything to worry about."

"So... you're not going to kill me?"

Tony laughed. She really had a lot to learn about him and his ways. "No. I'm not going to kill you."

"Hurt me?"

"No, I'm not going to hurt you. Why would I hurt such a wonderful lady?"

"Umm…maybe because you said so, and I believe that you would," she said as she stared at him.

"Well, I give you my word that you are safe."

"What about the others? Do they know?"

"The others know not to touch you in any way. They don't make that kind of move unless I say so," he stated. Tony and his crew knew not to make moves on each other's wives or girlfriends. If one even dared to do so, they would reap the consequences.

Mia released a sigh of relief. Things ended very differently than she thought. She was glad that this was over for her, but she still had Sean to worry about. "Thank you."

"Don't thank me yet. There's something else I want to tell you." This time he took a deep breath. He's been through so much more, but the thought of losing someone he's never had frightened him.

She prepared herself for what she was about to hear. Did things just get better just to get worse? "What is it?"

"Remember, I told you Sean wasn't the person you think he is?"

"Yeah, and you were right. Is there more?"

"Yeah, there's way more." He could feel Mia slowly pulling away from him. He was losing her. "Sean came to me with a proposition a while ago. He knew I wanted you, so he offered you to me."

"Wait…what? Why would he do that? I don't believe you," she said as she pulled away. "He would never do that to me." She began walking away.

"I caught him and Angela kissing." Saying those words made her stop in her tracks. He'd just confirmed what her heart already knew. "I told him he was out. He got mad and said he needed the work. I didn't care if he needed the work or not. So, he offered you, and I refused because I knew you were special and deserved more. He broke a promise to you, and by doing so, he showed me that he couldn't be trusted."

Mia said nothing as she opened the doors to the office and stormed out. She tore his shirt from her body, causing buttons to fly everywhere and immediately began putting on her clothes. She could hear Tony's voice behind her, trying to calm her down, but it wasn't working. She grabbed her purse and headed towards the bedroom door to let herself out.

"I almost forgot," she reached in her purse and pulled out five stacks of money. "I figured you wouldn't take a check," she said as she placed them on the dresser.

"You know you could have told me sooner."

"I didn't want to hurt you," he said as he grabbed her by the hand. He wanted to hold her, but he knew she would just pull away. "I'm sorry."

For some reason, she believed him. She didn't know what to say in return, so she said nothing. She didn't want to say anything out of anger that she would regret the next day. "I should get going." She let her hand slip out of his as he watched her walk away. She got to the door and stood there. Part of her wanted to leave while part of her wanted to stay. "Why did you tell me? You could have kept all this to yourself." Mia could hear his footsteps as he came closer.

He wanted to wrap his arms around her and hold her close, but he wanted his words to be the last thing she would remember, not his touch. "I didn't want any secret between us. If..... there was ever an us. You're the first woman to find a home in my heart. I know it's crazy to miss what I never had."

"You had me," she whispered.

"No, I never had you. I had your body, but not what makes you, you. I want all of you doll face."

The tears ran down Mia's face as she listened to every word that Tony had to say. She wanted to turn around and kiss him and tell him everything he wanted to hear, but instead, she left him standing there. She ran down the stairs and didn't stop until she was in the car, where she cried. These feelings that she was feeling shouldn't have happened. Was this all a mistake? She was falling in love with a Kingpin, and a Kingpin was falling in love with her. She was so caught up in her own affairs that she had forgotten all about Sean.

"Oh my gosh, Sean!"

CHAPTER SEVENTEEN

Tony sat in the passenger seat as his driver John also known as Dirty John. He arrived at an old warehouse where he used to conduct business. It was the same warehouse that Sean decided to conduct his business as well.

"I'm ready to get dirty," said Dirty John as he took his gun from under his seat and loaded it. "Ready boss?"

"Yeah," said Tony. His body was there, but his mind was a mile away. He had a sadness about him when he saw Mia walk away. Part of him wanted to run after her and kiss her until she had a change of heart, but he wanted her freely on her own. "Let's go," he stated as he opened his car door and got out. He missed Mia a little too much, but right now, he had even more important things to deal with. He was pissed and furious that another shipment was once again flagged by the Feds. Every time this happens, his merchandise is held up until the investigation is over.

"Yo, Tony!" Sal yelled as he greeted Tony with open arms. "What took so long?" he asked.

"Had to take care of things. Where is the asshole?"

"You mean assholes," said Sal. "Right this way. You won't believe who he had working for him."

They made their way from the car as they carefully glanced around. Even though their old stomping ground was familiar, they treated it as new while Tony's other men checked the perimeter. They always had to be careful. They knew never to let their guards down. There was always someone looking to take out the crew, especially Tony.

"Who else is here?" Tony asked.

"Danny and Rich are inside," said Sal.

"So, who's this other fool that tried to cross me?" Tony asked as they entered the building. To his surprise, he saw four chairs holding four familiar people. They were all tied with their hands behind their backs, and their mouth taped. Sean, Angela, Lil Nicky, and Jimmy. Ole Jimmy, he knew he shouldn't have trusted him, but never again.

"These are assholes that tried to cross you," said Sal as he pointed to them.

Tony stared at them before walking up to Jimmy first. He said nothing as he reached into his pocket and pulled out his brass knuckles. He placed them on his fingers. With great anger, he took his fist and rammed it into his face and stomach over and over until he saw blood. "Anything you wanna fucking say, Jimmy?" He said as he removed the tape from Jimmy's mouth.

As soon as Tony removed the tape, Jimmy spits out blood. He looked at Tony as if he wanted to kill him, yet he still wanted mercy. "I'm sorry, Tony. I just needed the extra money," he cried as he coughed up more blood. "I had no idea it was your money."

Tony really didn't want to hear anything that Jimmy had to say, but he wanted to be fair. He wanted to hear the reason why the two-timing low life would betray him. After all, he gave him a chance after being a convicted felon and gave him extra cash to help his family. He went against everything he believed in, and this is how Jimmy repays him.

"Tony!" Jimmy cried. "I'm sorry. I didn't mean to betray you, Tony. I'm sorry!"

Tony had enough of his whining. "Shut him up," he said to Sal. "You know Jimmy, I always knew you had sticky fingers, but I hoped you would keep them clean when working for me. I trusted you."

"Tony, no! Please, Tony," Jimmy begged as Sal taped his mouth up again.

Lil Nicky was next on Tony's list. "Nicky, Nicky, things could have been different for you. I gave you multiple chances, and this is how you repay me," he said as he snatched the tape from Lil Nicky's mouth.

Lil Nicky said nothing as he stared Tony in the eyes. He had nothing to say to him. He hated Tony and hated how he treated him. He was grown, but Tony always treated him like a kid. "I have nothing to say to you," Lil Nicky said as he spat near Tony's shoes. "I ain't no snitch!"

Tony looked down at the spit and back at Nicky with a smile on his face. He looked at Sal and John and laughed. "He's no snitch," he laughed.

"The kid got guts. That's for sure," said Sal.

"So will the floor," said John as he taped up Nicky's mouth.

Tony didn't bother to bang up Nicky like he did Jimmy. He had something else in mind. Something that will send a message to anyone that stole from him. He looked over at Angela. He could tell she was nervous. She was breathing heavily as her chest moved up and down. He didn't forget about her as he moved his attention to the ringleader, Sean.

"Sean, Sean, Sean," repeatedly he said as he snatched the tape from his mouth. "What should I do with you. I really thought we would be cool."

"Fuck you," said Sean. "We would never be cool. You're a fake, a wannabe." Sean loved to talk shit to Tony. He knew Tony wasn't like his father. His father had balls, and Tony didn't. He knew Tony didn't have the balls to kill anyone. The talk around town was all rumors, and he had nothing to fear. "You'll never be your father."

"And you'll never be me," he chuckled before swinging his fist across Sean's face. Back and forward, he went until he saw blood dripping from Sean's face. This was more than just business. This was now personal. How dare he bring up his father. After two more hits, Tony took a break. He stepped away and looked down at his bloody knuckles.

"Here you go, boss," said John as he handed Tony a towel to clean his hand.

Tony wiped his hands off, and the brass knuckles and placed it back into his pocket. He was through with the beatings. He needed to move on to the next step. The next step that no one saw coming.

"What should I do with you all? I think right now I'm being quite generous. Everyone is still breathing," he said as he looked at them. "John, would you do me the honors."

"The pleasure is all mine," said John as he reached into his back pocket and pulled out a pair of wire cutters. John wasn't called Dirty John for just for the hell of it. He enjoyed his job, maybe a little too much. He didn't mind getting his hands dirty, and whenever he got questioned by the cops, his hands were clean. He then walked over to Jimmy and snipped the tip of his fingers off.

Jimmy screams were muffled by the tape as he cried out from the pain. He wanted to run, but he knew running would only make things worse. He stared at Tony, hoping that he would have some type of mercy for him, but he was wrong.

"Sticky fingers Jimmy, they will always get you in trouble," said Tony.

Tony began putting the silencer on his gun. The look on everyone's face just got real. Angela knew Tony wasn't going to kill her. Women and children were off-limits, but Nicky wasn't a child anymore. She knew she couldn't save him even if she wanted to, but she will try. She stared at Tony and tried to mumble something, but only she understood. She was relieved when she felt the tape being ripped from her mouth. Everyone got a chance to say something, and now she wanted her turn.

"Tony…Tony don't do this, please," Angela begged. "I can pay you back. I promise Tony!"

"Somebody has to pay," he stated.

"It was all Sean. We didn't want to do it, Tony. He threatened us."

"Angela, sweetie, calm down. I'm not going to kill you. You know that's not what I'm known for."

"What about my son Tony? He's innocent. You gotta let him go too," she cried.

"Now, why would I do that? You two were the eyes of this whole operation. You all made sure Sean couldn't be caught. You all are just as guilty as he is."

"I'm sorry, Tony," cried Angela.

"Someone has to pay for your actions."

Tony stood there and listened to Angela ramble on about how it was all Sean's fault. She wanted him to let her and Nicky go. She begged, but Tony wasn't going for it. Somebody was going to pay. Letting them go free would only send a message of weakness, and he wasn't weak. He was the infamous Tony Spillane, and they were going to find out just how infamous he was.

"It was a mistake, Tony. It won't happen again, I promise," she sobbed.

"I know," Tony said as he took his time loading the gun. "You all will learn a valuable lesson today. I take our bond seriously, and if anyone breaks it, they send dishonor towards our name and what we stand for. We are a family here. We are unbreakable. The only way out is death." Tony continued with his speech as their cries could be heard in a muffle from under the tape. Suddenly their cries slowly subsided as they stared at the door.

Tony turned around to see what everyone was staring at. His world stopped when he saw his heart standing in the opening. He knew then he would have to change the game, but even if he did, someone still had to die.

CHAPTER EIGHTEEN

Mia stood in the doorway of the warehouse. She was frightened of the sight before her. Four individuals sat tied up with fear in their eyes. The sight before her was unreal. Was this the Tony everyone talked about because lately, this wasn't the guy she saw. She walked closer but stopped when she saw the pool of blood under Jimmy's chair.

"Oh God!" she gasped as she placed her hand over her mouth.

"What are you doing here?" Tony asked as he walked closer to her. He saw her glimpsed at the gun in his hand and took a step back. He didn't want her to be afraid of him, so he gave the gun to Sal. "How did you find me?"

"I followed you, but now I'm sorry that I did," she said as she looked at them. "What are you doing to them? You can't do this, it's wrong."

"What's wrong is they stole from me and expected to walk free. Nobody takes from me!"

"There's got to be another way, Tony. This isn't you."

"You don't know me," he said with a rough tone.

"Maybe I don't, but I do know this isn't the man that I came to know these last few days. Whatever happened to that, Tony?"

"You have a lot to learn doll face," he said as he began to walk away but stopped when Mia grabbed his hand. Her hands were soft against his hand and reminded him of the rest of her body. "You should leave."

"I can't unless the man I've fallen for is coming with me right now."

Tony turned to Mia. How could she still love a man that was unfaithful to her? Sean didn't deserve her. He was a liar, a thief, and a cheater. A bad combination all around, no matter how you look at it. "You should go."

"If I do, what will happen to Sean?"

"You're still trying to fight his battles. You hear that, Sean!" He called out to Sean before walking up to him and ripping the tape off his mouth. "Your woman here is still fighting your battles."

"Mia, go home!" Sean yells breathlessly.

She could tell he was in pain, worse than before. She couldn't stand seeing him like that and began to cry. "I'm sorry, Sean," she said as she ran to him and kneeled in front of him.

"It's ok baby. Everything will be ok. I got this."

"Shut up," she cried. "Just shut up, ok!"

"Baby, I'm sorry ok. I'm sorry for everything. Just know I love you, and when this is over, we will get married and move on with our life."

"No," said Mia as she shook her head. "I know about the affair, Sean. I know everything."

"What? Baby, it was one time. She meant nothing to me. I promise things will be different," said Sean as he tried to plead his case, but it was too late.

"Fuck you!" Angela yelled.

"Shut up, Angela!" Sean yelled back. "Mia… baby, please. I love you!"

"Just shut up, Sean!" She yelled. "You never listen. All you had to do was listen, and we wouldn't be in this situation. I wouldn't have to choose."

"What do you mean you wouldn't have to choose?" The way he stared at Mia made her leave her stance and stood up. "Baby…what do you mean? Talk to me!"

Now he wanted to talk, but it was a little too late for talking. "I'm sorry. I need more than what you can give me. I need honesty, loyalty, and trust. You broke them all, and now I…I don't know if it's fixable Sean."

After hearing those words, Sean launched at Mia

but was held back by the strong arms of Sal. "You're leaving me? Baby, I thought we were in this together? Huh! Those were your words."

"We were until you kept me in the dark," she said as she looked at Angela. Mia wiped her eyes and went to stand by Tony.

"So, you with him now?" Sean asked.

Mia looked at Sean and fed him the same words that he once said to her. "Some things are better left unsaid."

Tony's face was blank with emotion, but inside he was smiling. Mia pulled a fast one on them both. He had no reason not to believe her intentions. He placed a hand around her waist and pulled her close and whispered in her ear.

"You should leave. You don't want to be here," said Tony.

"What will happen to him?" She whispered.

"Leave while you can. I don't want you involved in anything that will happen here tonight. It could get ugly quick."

Mia looked back at Sean. She wanted to run to him and hold him. She wanted to tell him she still loved him, but every time she thought about it, the thought of him and Angela would cross her mind.

"Wait outside for me," said Tony.

"What about Sean?"

"Just go," Tony demanded.

Mia did as she was told. She waited outside with a heavy heart as the tears slid down her cheeks. She shouldn't feel this way, but she did. This was all Sean's fault. She didn't ask for any of this, but somehow, she felt she was to blame. After five minutes of waiting, suddenly, her heart dropped as the sound of screams filled the air, followed by gunshots. She waited a minute too long and couldn't stay any longer. She began walking away with her heart dragging behind her. It was over. Everything was over.

"What have I done," she whispered as she got in her car and drove away.

CHAPTER NINETEEN

Mia sat at her desk in her office, doing paperwork. Lately, it's all she's been doing while trying to act as normal as possible. It's been three weeks since having any contact with Tony and Sean. She started to leave town but didn't want to look suspicious of Sean's disappearance. She wanted to go to the police and tell them everything that went on, but she was scared that somehow, they were on Tony's payroll. So instead, she kept a low profile so she wouldn't have to answer any questions. The only person that knew part of the story was her friend Kayla.

Her mind then drifted back on her and Tony. Deep down inside, she wanted to get to know the man behind the mask. She missed him and everything about him. The way he held her and the way he kissed her. While being around him, Tony made her feel like everything was going to be ok. Even though the timing was wrong, she couldn't help but feel that the timing was right. After all, she should feel thankful. If it wasn't for Tony, she wouldn't have known Sean's true colors.

Mia's thoughts were scattered as her cellphone began ringing. She opened the top drawer to her desk and looked at the number that was calling. It was an unfamiliar number that she didn't know. Calls like these, she tended not to answer. It was probably a spam caller anyway, so she hit the ignore button.

"Damn spam caller," she said aloud as she continued working.

Her phone began ringing, again and again, she hit the ignore button. It wasn't until the third call that she began to get irritated. This time she planned to answer the phone and let whoever was calling her have it. Today just wasn't the day.

"Hello!" She yelled. No one said anything. She was about to hang up until she heard the recording message playing.

Caller: You have a collect call from Sean. An inmate at Shelby County Correction Facility. The call will be recorded at any time. If you wish to accept this call, press five.

Mia did nothing. Instead, she hung up. She quickly brought up the website to see if what she just heard was true. She then keyed in Sean's name, and to her surprise, he was there in jail with drug-related charges. Tears of joy began building up in her eyes. She should have talked to him but thought it was best this way, at least for now. She couldn't stop smiling at the good news. The entire time she was worried and thought the worst had happened to him. Now that she had answers, she was finally comfortable to handle the questions behind Sean's disappearance, if any, was asked.

A knock came at her door that interrupted her joy. She quickly wiped her eyes. She didn't need any of her co-workers or employees in her business. "Come in," she called out as she pretended to be working. As the door opened, she looked up to see the man she's been craving since she left his bed.

"Hello doll face," Tony said as he walked in and closed the door behind him.

"Tony?" She said as she stood up from her desk. She didn't know if she should be happy or upset as she saw him standing there. No matter how much she wanted to be mad, it was hard when parts of her body seemed to be craving his touch. She wanted to play it cool, but she couldn't help herself. She ran from behind her desk and threw herself into his arms. Out of all the other times, this was the first time she was truly sincerely happy to see him.

Tony didn't know how she would feel about seeing him as he wrapped both arms around her and held her close. He pulled away just enough to look her in the eyes. "You've been crying," he said.

"Just a little," Mia said as she smiled. "They're happy tears."

"Happy to see me or something else?"

"Actually, a little bit of both. I just received a collect call from someone. Why did you have me to believe that

Sean was dead?"

"I never wanted you to believe that. You were supposed to have waited on me. I wanted to explain everything to you afterward, but when I came out, you were gone. I stopped by your house, but you were not there. I tried to call you, but you didn't answer your phone. I figured I would give you time to yourself."

"You could have left me a voicemail," she stated.

"Something like that, you don't leave on a voicemail sweetheart, so here I am now telling you," he stated as Mia hugged him again.

"Thank you," she said.

"I also came because I wanted to see you. I've missed you. You're so different than me, yet I feel that you complete me. I want you."

"I want you too," said Mia without hesitation. That was all it took before Tony gathered her up in his arms and placed her on her desk.

He kissed her as his hands wandered down to her ass where he cuffed the bottom. He then laid her down with her back against her desk as he opened her blouse. He began fondling her breasts while kissing each nipple. He hiked up her skirt and pulled her panty aside. He then slipped in two fingers while his thumb massaged her clit.

Once again, Mia laid in pure ecstasy as she heard his zipper being unzipped. She prepared herself for his entrance as she felt the tip go in. She gasped at the size.

No matter how prepared she thought she was, she was never prepared for the size of him. He loved her with every stroke as he moved in and out. She wrapped her legs around him and pulled him in closer. She wanted to feel all of him and didn't want anything holding him back.

Tony couldn't take anymore as his pace increased. She knew he was close as he pounded her good. She removed her legs from around his waist to give him room to pull out, but instead, he kept going until he spilled his seed inside. He slid his arms under her and held her close until his heavy breathing subsided.

"Tony," she whispered. "Remember that day when I said I wasn't going to leave until the person that I've fallen for was coming too?"

"Yeah, what about it."

"Well, I was talking about you."

"How can you be so sure?"

"I just know," she stated.

"There's no way someone like you could love someone like me. I live a complicated life, and there are times where I have to do the unthinkable," he said as he looked at her. He got up from his position and pulled her up with him. He held her close as he looked her in the eyes. "The life I live isn't a game. I'm not talking marriage anytime soon, but if you have me as your man, just know that I'm not a saint, but I'm definitely not a cheater."

"As long as you are honest and loyal, I think I can

handle the rest."

"I sure hope you can too because I'm definitely not perfect. Loyal and honest, that I can be," he stated.

"Nobody's perfect, right?"

"Right," he said as he kissed her again. "I knew there was something about you when I first laid eyes on you, and now I have you all to myself." He kissed her again and gave her ass a squeeze before finally pulling himself away. He loved her ass. The roundness and fullness of it made him go crazy. "I have a meeting to attend."

"Will I see you tonight?" she asked.

"You can see me any night or every night. Where have you been staying if you're not staying at your place?" he asked as he got himself together.

"I've been staying with my friend Kayla," she said as she buttoned up her top and smoothed her skirt down.

"Here."

Mia looked up to see Tony taking a key from off his keyring.

"What's that for?" she asked curiously.

"It's the key to my penthouse. You can stay there until you feel like moving back into your place."

"She thought about it before taking the key. "Thank you," she said.

"I gotta go doll face, but I'll see you tonight." Tony kissed her one last time before leaving out the door.

Mia didn't say anything as she looked down at her hand, holding the key. She hurried to freshen up in the bathroom located inside of her office before getting back to work. She smiled at the thought that played over in her head. Who would have known the outcome would end like this. She was now dating the infamous Tony Spillane. She was now Tony's girl.